The Chair 2

By R. R. Sechi

1.

Paul Dickens arrived at the entrance to Willowbrook and grimaced as he regarded the wrought iron gates now hanging dejectedly from their hinges. *Bloody vandals*, he thought, *just what I needed.* He had been the caretaker there for a number of years now and only usually checked on the place once a quarter and generally there was not much to do; which was the way he liked it. However, from time to time, these things inevitably happened.

He got back in his car, slamming the door moodily behind him and proceeded to drive down the winding track that led to the old institution in the vague hope of catching the culprit(s). Reaching the top of a slight incline in the road, the dilapidated building came into view, looming proud in its neglect. Also, he caught sight of a car parked outside and so he sped up thinking for once he just might, apprehend somebody.

Parking alongside the vehicle, he got out and approached the main entrance doors which were slightly ajar; the Saturday afternoon breeze whistling tunelessly through the eaves of old Willowbrook. It was a downcast day and Dickens shivered as he neared the doorway; it wasn't just the weather though; this place always gave him the creeps. He paused at the entrance and scratched his silvery beard in silent contemplation; *maybe he should call the police.* Paul quickly dismissed the idea as he knew from experience they would not consider acts of vandalism as a high priority and would probably take at least an hour to turn up; by which time the culprits would be long gone.

Retrieving his pocket flashlight from his jacket he proceeded inside. The ground floor was expectedly gloomy but some light managed to penetrate through the gaps in the boarded-up windows and he could see without much difficulty. He systematically began to check all the rooms on that level being careful to avoid as much of the fallen debris as he could, to limit the noise that he made. *He didn't want to scare the buggers off, after all.*

A while later, he was satisfied that they were all empty and made a mental note to himself to replace some of the boards on the windows, which he had noticed had come loose or fallen off. Entering the stairwell, he considered the option of checking the basement first but decided against, as he knew it would be pitch black down there and most likely the intruders would have gone upstairs; that's how he justified it to himself anyway.

Wheezing slightly as he climbed, he paused at several of the landings to catch his breath. Dickens was in his early sixties and hoping to retire in the next few years with any luck. *Best not think about that now, I've got a job to do*, he thought. Reaching the second floor, he opened the stairwell door which yielded with a rusted creaking grating noise on the cold stone floor. Luckily, the windows were not boarded on this level as there was no need and visibility was much better.

Following the various corridors, he checked the rooms one-by-one, his footsteps giving off a dull echo as he walked. All he found was the usual rusted bed frames and spoilt remains of mattresses and dilapidated furniture. *No-one was there.* Dickens went back to the stairwell and headed down to check the first floor. After another fruitless search of the rooms there, he returned to the ground level and grimaced at the thought that he'd now have to check the basement.

Flicking on his flashlight he proceeded down into the thickening gloom which seemed to get darker with every step. He could hear a loud dripping noise from somewhere in the distance which chilled him.

His feet crunched on fallen debris and he nearly stumbled and fell at one point, but just managed to regain his footing. His sixth sense was now screaming within him to abandon this mission and get out as fast as he could, before it was *too late.*

Dickens did his best to ignore it and with some difficulty he continued his descent. Soon a foul smell seemed to permeate and fill his nostrils which became worse as he proceeded down. The darkness enveloped him and he shuddered and felt chilled to the bone, his hairs standing on end at the back of his neck. He prayed his batteries would not give out, as he would be totally blind without the dim light source to guide him.

Finally, Dickens reached the bottom and nearly gagged at the hideously potent smell emanating from somewhere close by. Feeling the urge to flee once more he wrestled open the basement door which screeched and groaned loudly in protest as it gave way. He paused for a second to let the sound dissipate and also to check that he was alone. All he could make out was that intermittent dripping noise which invaded the otherwise dead silence.

He covered his mouth and nose with a pocket handkerchief in a vain attempt to limit the foul corrupt air that he was breathing in, and proceeded down the corridor, shining his flashlight into the cells as he went. Everything appeared to be charred or scorched from the conflagration that had decimated the place some decades earlier. Dickens footsteps crunched on debris and echoed around the confined space as he walked, even though he did his best to tread carefully, to limit the noise that he was making.

The first two cells were empty with just charred metal bed frames and broken latrines, as other furnishings must have been destroyed by the fire. Dickens was now constantly gagging, as he battled to carry on, as the smell was so hideously vile, dank and corrupt. Reaching the third cell, he shone the flashlight inside, and gasped in horror as the light beam happened to focus directly on the chair and the broken skeleton that sat back on it; a few pieces of rotting tissue still remained adorning it.

He shone the light around the room and saw another skeleton nearby on the floor, it too having some last morsels of corrupted flesh hanging from it. His heart hammered in his chest when a large black furry rat scurried from view into a dark corner. *Oh my God*, he thought, *what happened here?* Dickens cautiously entered the room and immediately grimaced when he stepped on the metallic door which lay on the floor across his path; it clanked and echoed loudly around the dark interior. Pausing, he stopped for breath as the menacing sound penetrated the bleak darkness all around him.

More careful this time, in regard to his footing, he stepped gingerly over towards the chair and the skeleton sitting almost upright back on it. In the faint light he could see that it was still wearing a diamond studded necklace in the shape of a cross. Surveying the floor nearby he suddenly spotted a ring that must have fallen from the corpse's finger. It too was composed of diamonds which glittered and sparkled in the faint light as he stooped and picked it up.

Without thinking, Dickens quickly pocketed the ring and then carefully removed the necklace from the skeleton's shoulders. The skull was resting on the back of the chair so he had to move it slightly forward, so he could lift the necklace over it. As he did so, he gagged again, as one of his fingers must have touched a loose remnant of rotting flesh which felt vile and corrupt to his touch. Consequently, he lost his grip on the skull and the whole skeleton clattered and fell from the chair into a heap in front

of it. The sound of bone on stone filled the air and echoed all around the dank dark interior.
Sweating profusely now, Dickens waited for the sound to dissipate. After it was gone, he paused for a while before moving, just in case. *Luckily,* he thought, *no-one else must be down here!* Next he regarded the other skeleton which lay nearby, for any signs of jewellery and was happy to relieve it too of a gold necklace and bangle. He patiently checked the floor all around the room, as he did not want to miss anything. *These jewels will certainly help add to my retirement fund,* he thought greedily. Satisfied that nothing else remained he decided to make a hasty exit. *All in all though not bad for an afternoon's work!*
Just as he was about to leave the cell, a piercing scream echoed down the corridor, originating from somewhere close by. Warm pee began to trickle down his trouser leg as fear gripped him and his brain acknowledged that it did not sound human. Frantically in a mindless panic he rushed towards the doorway, forgetting that the metallic door lay on the floor across his path. He stumbled over it and fell, landing heavily on one knee, and cried out in pain and agony as he did so.
The creature whatever it was answered him with a fierce shrill cry of menace of its own, this time much louder. Dickens could now hear its heavy footsteps crunching on the loose debris as it ventured towards him. Luckily, he had kept a tight grip on the flashlight and not dropped it; as instinctively he'd known his life might depend on it. He tried to rise to his feet but his right leg gave out, and he immediately fell back down in agony. However, the inhuman being's approach spurred him to begin to crawl, as best as he could, towards the doorway in the vain hope of reaching the exit and freedom.

Dickens made it as far as the corridor and was just about to head towards the exit when he felt the being's claws thrust into the small of his back. He screamed in excruciating pain and suffering as it lifted him from the stone floor. Its hot foul breath seemed to burn the back of his neck as it lifted him from behind, high into the air. Surprisingly though, he found that he was still holding the flashlight and to his horror, the creature removed one of its claws from his back and brought it round in front of his face.

In the dim flashlight he could see it had black charred skin and penetratingly long hideous nails on the tips of its claws. Dickens in his abject fear and agony, had a lucid moment of time standing still and seemingly passing slower, moment by moment. He could see that in the creature's claw it held a dagger, the handle of which was composed of three intertwining snakes that shone like emeralds and appeared to be elevated as though they might reach out and bite you. His last thought was watching this strange dagger swipe across his throat and feeling his lifeblood gushing out before him, before he was floating away out of existence.

Police officer Lauren Mitchell and her colleague Kristen Gallagher were out on patrol in their squad car. It was a boring Sunday afternoon, with not much to do, but just drive around and show a presence to reassure the community that they were out doing their job. Lauren was in her late twenties and by all accounts extremely attractive with long blond hair which she tied up in a bob whilst on duty. In contrast Kristen had short dark hair and very masculine looks which made her prone to numerous lesbian jibes back at the station.

The two of them had been partnered for just over a year now and had developed a good professional if not exactly great personal relationship. They were still both getting over Kristen making a pass at Lauren one fateful day, about six months ago which she'd rejected and the rest was history. What got to Lauren though the most was that Kristen claimed not to be gay and just bi-curious; *whatever that meant.* Anyway, it was some time ago now and they both had worked hard on developing a strictly professional and platonic relationship.

For the last few hours they had been driving around with very little to do and not much in the way of conversation either. Just then a call came through from dispatch on the radio: "Any available unit, we have a reported misper (missing person), a Paul Dickens, age 62, long silver hair with beard, medium build, wearing a light coloured top, dark jacket and brown trousers. He was last known to be visiting the old Willowbrook mental institution yesterday afternoon and has not been seen since."

Kristen replied on the radio as Lauren was driving: "This is Lima-Charlie 76 (LC76) we're in the area and will check it out over."

"Assigning you now, LC76 over", finished the dispatcher.

Lauren nodded at Kristen and headed towards the old mental institution. They rarely patrolled that way, as it was out in the middle of nowhere and not a particular place of concern. However, from time-to-time the odd call came through, mainly vandal related though and they or a fellow unit would attend.

"Think the last time we went there was eight or nine months ago, just a complete waste of time", said Kristen moodily.

"Yeah, too true but at least it's something to do besides just drive around", Lauren replied nonchalantly.

Arriving at Willowbrook they cruised past the broken entrance gates acknowledging that at least it appeared that something was amiss, and Lauren headed towards the main building down the winding track. Reaching Willowbrook they radioed in the two registration plates of the vehicles parked there and awaited a response.

"LC76, we have confirmation one vehicle is registered to misper Paul Dickens and the other to a Jess Anderson, also a misper and potential murder suspect", the dispatcher responded matter-of-factly.

On hearing the latter Kristen immediately replied on the radio, "LC76- requesting backup when available over."

Moments later the response from headquarters came through: "LC76- all units currently engaged but will send you backup ASAP, over."

Lauren shrugged, "Okay, let's have a look inside."

Kristen nodded and they got out of the patrol car and headed towards the old mental institution. Removing their flashlights from their belts they proceeded inside through the main doors which were slightly ajar. The ground floor was dull and gloomy as they set about their search. After checking all the rooms on that level and finding nothing they headed for the stairwell that they'd both noticed earlier.

The door yielded with a grating creak which made them both grimace as they surveyed the options: up or down. "Let's check the basement first", said Kristen, "I just caught a horrible whiff of something coming up from there." Lauren nodded and they proceeded down carefully avoiding much of the fallen debris as best as they could.

As they descended the stairs, the vile smell seemed to both corrupt and inhibit their senses and at times they both found themselves nearly gagging or retching. Into the darkness they went, but their flashlights were strong and powerful and did much to penetrate the ever-present gloom all around them. At the bottom, they forced open the door which yielded with a metallic grating creak that echoed menacingly all around them. Taking a moment, they waited until the sound had dissipated before proceeding on.

They quickly checked a few vacant cells before coming across a body directly in their path lying within the corridor. A multitude of hairy bodies covered it feasting on the remains. Kristen took out her gun and fired it above the multitude of rats which were feasting there, which quickly scurried off in all directions to any dark corners available. The gunshot echoed interminably around the confined space for some time afterwards.

The two officers approached and grimaced at the half-eaten corpse but could easily confirm that it was definitely the misper Paul Dickens judging by his hair, build and clothing. Lauren retched and nearly threw up on seeing Dickens's half-eaten face. Kristen immediately tried her radio but couldn't get a signal down in the basement.

She was about to head back up the way they had come when Lauren stopped her, "Let's finish our search down here, then we'll call it in, okay?"

Her partner looked indecisive for once, but nodded her acquiescence and they gingerly stepped over the body, trying to avoid the pool of blood and peered into the nearby cell on their right. Horror struck them forcibly once more as they saw the chair and the two skeletons lying on the floor beside it both with bits of rotting flesh hanging from them. A scene so macabre it called on any sane person to despair.

Enough was enough and Lauren decisively stated, "Okay, we've got multiple possible homicides, let's get out of here and call it in."

Kristen was only too willing to agree, and they headed out as fast as they could, both determinedly

trying to escape the scene of horror and vile smell which emanated so powerfully from down there. As they ascended the stairwell they again both gagged and retched as their bodies desperately tried to dispel the foulness from their insides. Helping each other, almost arm-in-arm, they continued upwards to escape this newly found nightmare.
Coughing and spluttering, they emerged into the fresh late afternoon air outside the entrance to Willowbrook, and they both took a few minutes to regain their senses and composure before Kristen called in the potential homicides via the radio.

Within the next hour, police arrived at the scene en masse, and a multitude of squad and forensics vehicles were soon parked up outside. The bodies were removed by the coroner's office and taken to the morgue where a post-mortem was to be carried out on Paul Dickens, even though the cause of death was clear- his throat had been slit ear-to-ear. Further, DNA could be taken from the tiny fragments of flesh on the skeletons to establish who they were but it seemed more than likely, due to the vehicle found there, that it was Jess Anderson and Sarah Hurd who had gone missing some three months earlier. Both of these females had been mispers and potential murder suspects.
The crime scene was quickly taped off and the main gates repaired, to keep out any unwanted attention. Some members of the press had caught wind of the story and were now being prevented from entry at the main entrance to the site. All the police officers had been instructed to make no comment to the media by their superiors, but clearly some leak had taken place within the department's ranks.
A cute slim brunette positioned herself in front of her camera crew to film the breaking story for DBEYH (don't believe everything you hear) news: -

'This is Sandy Shaw reporting outside the old Willowbrook mental institution where late this afternoon at least three bodies have been recovered. One of the deceased is believed to be a Jess Anderson, a former missing person and suspect in the infamous Anderson murder case where her husband John and two senior police officers, as well as a family friend, a Rick Clay, were found brutally murdered at the Anderson's home. Also the body of another potential murder suspect, a Sarah Hurd, a close friend of Mrs Anderson is also believed to be among those found here today. That's all we have for the moment but stay tuned for regular updates as they come in.'

Sandy finished her live report and addressed one of her colleagues, James Sanders with disdain, "Jimmy is that all you've got for me? C'mon, get to work this story is going to be big- I can feel it!" she finished brushing past him and heading back to the news-van before he could even reply.

Shortly afterwards, the case was taken on by the homicide division and officers Lauren Mitchell and Kristen Gallagher resumed their normal duties. After an extensive investigation the case was closed pending further evidence, as there were literally no leads to go on. The bodies of Jess Anderson, Sarah Hurd and Paul Dickens were confirmed as the deceased. However, there was no possible motive or reason why these events had transpired, as well as the horrific events that occurred some three months earlier, at the Anderson's home.
Even though the case had been shelved, the various news reports regarding the incident had created quite a storm of interest via the internet and general media. There was nothing like some gruesome deaths to spark the public interest, or so it seemed. However, after a while such speculations fizzled out

into nothingness as other stories hit the headlines and Willowbrook became once again, almost forgotten, as yesterday's news.

2.

A few months later, around 10pm, a van pulled up outside the repaired gates to the old Willowbrook mental institution. A figure dressed in black, exited the van and headed over to the gates, with a pair of heavy-duty bolt-cutters and removed the locks and chains from their bindings. Opening them wide, so that the van could pass, the figure then replaced some of the chains to make it appear as though everything was normal and carefully closed them together, before getting back into the vehicle which then proceeded on.
Shortly afterwards, the van parked up outside the main entrance to Willowbrook and a number of people all dressed in black got out and approached the building which was still plastered at ground level with police tape- *do not cross*. They paused in a group together at the main door as one of them signalled the others with his hand to gather round.
“Okay guys let’s do the initial sequence here, before we go in”, said Chris, nodding towards Sam and Lee who had the hand-held video cameras. The remainder of their entourage Megan, Charlie and Beth sorted out the sound and the lighting between them and when all were ready they began to film:-

‘Here we are for a night vigil at the infamous Willowbrook mental institution, the scene of countless horrors and multiple deaths, many via an electric chair that we believe to this day is still here!’ Chris began pausing for effect, his face menacing under the portable battery-powered lights. *‘Even before we go in I sense that this is going to be a night to remember, I can just feel it! How can we not expect some paranormal activity at the scene of so many*

gruesome incidents! Come with us tonight as we explore Willowbrook in the dead of night!'

"Okay, cut", Chris finished before continuing, "That's the intro sorted... Guys, get the rest of the equipment out of the van and let's set up inside, no time to waste- let's move it people!"

An onerous groan of thunder sounded in the distance as the rest of the group headed over to unload the van and bring all the various sensors and monitoring equipment inside. The moonlight aided their quest somewhat even though a stiffening breeze began to chill them to the bone. It looked as though a storm was coming, so even more reason to make haste and get the expensive electronic devices indoors and out of any potential rain.

Soon afterwards, they were all assembled inside and were busy checking over their equipment using the glare from some portable lights that they had placed in the foyer. Beyond the lights, the dark was deep, black and absolute nothingness. The team were from a small cable TV channel that did reports on paranormal activity in the ever-present hope of seeing or witnessing some ghostly apparitions or unexplained sightings.

"Okay Megan and Beth, you take the first floor... Charlie and Lee the second and Sam you come with me- we're going to check out the basement! Remember, keep in touch on your radios with any reports or sightings and as the night goes on we can change places and floors. Are we all set? Yes- okay let's move like we've got a purpose!" Chris finished as he headed towards the stairwell with Sam in tow. Luckily, the overhead signs in the corridors were still fairly visible and using their flashlights they managed to locate the stairs and proceed down, both carrying cases of equipment with them. Shortly afterwards, Megan and Beth followed them but headed upstairs, with Lee and Charlie slightly lagging behind who would take the first floor as planned.

"I just know we're going to get some mega-footage tonight!" Chris almost shouted in his exuberance with Sam following behind him in quiet contemplation, and if she was honest, growing trepidation and fear. They headed down into the gloomy darkness with their flashlights constantly battling to keep back the shadows from invading their territory. Soon the lingering remnants of foul corrupt dank vileness assaulted their senses and both of them nearly gagged at the hideous smell.

"Breathe through your mouth, not your nose", Chris advised her and Sam just nodded in between sudden bouts of choking. Her body clearly was objecting to the circumstances and even though she hated to admit it, her mind was too. She just wanted to get out of there and as soon as possible!

Ignoring her sixth sense, she followed Chris down into the void until they reached the bottom where they forced the basement door open which yielded with a grating clanking creaking sound which reverberated and echoed all around the confined space. Even with all his current enthusiasm, Chris paused and waited for the noise to dissipate before proceeding inside.

The dank vile air assaulted and chilled them simultaneously. Sam followed Chris as he checked the two first cells but both were empty and he continued down the corridor. He shone his light into the third cell and cried out, "Bingo! I can't believe it... the chair is still here! Check it out Sam", he finished entering the cell. She did as instructed and was soon confronted by the malevolent chair. Sam shuddered thinking how many people had died on it in painful agony.

"Okay, let's get the equipment set up in here", Chris said, whilst turning on a portable battery-powered lamp.

Sam tested her sensor, which measured minute changes in air pressure and density scanning the room as she did so. "I'm getting readings off the scale", she said bemused, "Maybe it's broken", she finished shaking the hand-held device in her hand.
"Let me see", Chris insisted. "Yeah that's really weird but then again look where we are- I just know we're going to get some great footage tonight! C'mon let's finish setting up."
Sam quietly did as she was instructed and turned on various monitors, sensors and recording equipment which they placed around the edges of the room. Fifteen minutes later they were ready to go. Chris got on his radio and spoke on their chosen frequency: "Megan, Beth do you read over?"
"Loud and clear", Beth replied momentarily.
"How are you girls doing?"
"Yeah, just about all set. Not really getting much in the way of readings as yet, but there's definitely a negative atmosphere", Megan added.
"Lee, Charlie- how are you doing?" inquired Chris.
"Yeah, cool man we're ready here- getting some odd readings too", answered Lee.
"Okay great let's start filming and get on the radio immediately, if you see or encounter anything interesting, over", finished Chris as the others replied in the affirmative.
Sam was ready to start recording with the video camera. "Shall I begin?" she asked.
Chris nodded and described the scene to the viewer:-

'Here we are in the basement of Willowbrook mental institution for the first night of our vigil. The atmosphere is electric"; he smiled whilst pointing over towards the chair at the back of the cell before continuing, *"It's hard to believe we're actually here at the scene of so many countless horrors, torture and death... We're already getting readings off the*

scale, so I'm sure when we switch to night vision we'll get some interesting activity. I'm here with Sam whilst Megan and Beth are currently occupying the second floor and Lee and Charlie the first and we'll be checking back with them soon.'

Chris paused and moved over towards the chair, *'So here it is the infamous chair! It certainly gives me the creeps! Now we know many people have died on it through the use of electro-shock therapy in the distant past, but then there was the more recent Anderson case that's been all over the news... A John and Jess Anderson were suspected of taking the chair to their family home and somehow through circumstances unknown, they have both now died. Also, two close friends of theirs, Sarah Hurd and a Rick Clay, as well as a number of police officers are believed to have died in connection with the subsequent events that transpired at that house... Did this chair have anything to do with the case? Yes, I suspect so...'*

Sam watched through the viewfinder as Chris paused for effect and then sat down on the chair to continue with his introduction. Strangely, he suddenly disappeared from view; bemused she looked away from the camera and towards the chair which was now empty. Quickly turning around, in case he was pulling a prank on her, she scanned the room but it was empty apart from the numerous items of equipment. Her heart hammered within her chest, as she looked dumbfoundedly around her in mesmerised incomprehension. "Fuck!" was the only word she could muster.

Chris regained consciousness from what he believed to be a very strange dream to find that he was riding a motorbike at high speed. His head was resting more or less on the fuel tank to limit the air flow over him. Peering through the visor of his helmet in such a crouched position as he found himself, offered limited visibility as the landscape rushed by. Also, he realised that he was dressed totally in leathers with hard patted gloves protecting his hands.

Wow, what a rush! He looked at the speed dial and could see that he was currently doing over 100mph. The weird thing was that he didn't know how to ride a motorbike and yet here he was seemingly doing it. Not just that though, but he did not seem to be consciously making the decisions on how much to turn the throttle and accelerate, or when to break or change gear. It appeared that he was just a passenger along for the ride, seeing through this other person's eyes with no choice in the matter. *Well, I might as well enjoy myself then, as who knew when or how long this dream or trip, may last*, he thought.

The road he was on had numerous bends, and he found himself constantly leaning over the side of the bike as he raced around the corners at high speed. Soon, Chris found that he was really beginning to love the feeling of oneness with the elements and surroundings and the exhilaration from the rapid acceleration. As he overtook numerous cars along the way, he grinned at the thought of how slow moving they appeared to be, compared to him.

Suddenly, he found that he was signalling to turn off the freeway or motorway that he was currently on, and shortly afterwards he found himself riding some deserted country roads with very little traffic. Consequently, soon he found that he was once again doing excessive speeds and having to shift his body-weight from one side of the bike to the other at the numerous corners. This he didn't like so much as *how could you know what you might encounter when travelling at high speed around blind bends?*

Chris was beginning to feel scared for the first time, as whoever was really in control of this bike, he recognised that it was clearly going way too fast, that was for sure. He wished the rider would slow down but if anything as soon as the thought entered his mind the opposite seemed to happen, and they accelerated even faster. He could even feel his knees scraping on the tarmac around bends as well as the slight brush from hedgerows on the side of the road.

Slow down for Heaven's sake! Almost praying now, he watched as they rounded a very sharp bend at high speed and looked on in horror, as a tractor suddenly pulled out into the road in front of them. Whoever was in control of the bike tried to avoid this large obstacle as best as he could, but was ultimately going to fast to be able to do so. Soon Chris felt excruciating pain as he realised the bike was sliding along the road on its side with one of his legs trapped beneath it. Luckily, the pain was momentary as he was crushed pummelled and flattened instantaneously under the huge back wheels of the tractor.

"Guys, we've got a situation here, you'd better get down and take a look", said Sam nervously via the radio, unsure of what else to do. One thing she knew for sure though was that she didn't want to be alone down there. "Do you read, over?" she finished.

"Hey Sam, what's the problem? Did you guys see anything?" Lee inquired.

"What's happened Sam?" added Beth.

"Guys, you need to come and see for yourself- I still can't believe it myself- Chris sat on the chair and vanished into thin air!" Sam answered dumbfoundedly.

"What? Are you kidding me?" Lee replied indignantly, "Chris is just messing you around,

that's all- don't wet yourself!" he finished laughing with Charlie clearly chastising her too inaudibly in the background.
"Take it easy Sam, I'm on my way", said Beth consolingly as she could tell her friend was scared out of her wits, and struggling to deal with the situation, whatever it was.
"Okay, cry-baby, I'm coming too", said Lee rebukingly.
Beth and Lee separately made their way down to the basement leaving Megan and Charlie manning the equipment on their respective floors. Five minutes later, Beth and Lee joined Sam in the basement who was looking disconsolate and Chris was nowhere in sight. Beth went over to Sam and took her in her arms in a comforting gesture and soon her friend was sobbing profusely.
Lee grimaced at the sight of them and stated coldly, "I'll check around, see where the idiot's gone to", before heading off down the corridor.
Beth was pretty and slim with her long brown hair tied up in a ponytail behind her, which contrasted sharply with Sam who was borderline obese with puffed out features and layers of fat all over her body, which she tried desperately to hide with large loose fitting clothing. Unfortunately, her choice just seemed to accentuate her lack of fitness rather than anything else.

Lee wandered down the corridor cursing under his breath at what he termed the *stupid fat bitch* or alternatively the *stupid fat fuck*. Why Chris had let the *dumb cow* join their group was a complete mystery to him, but then he knew that Chris had a thing for Beth, and Sam was her friend so say no more. His trainers crunched on the fallen debris as he traversed the corridor checking the basement cell-by-cell. All he found was rottenness, charred remains and decay in the rest of the thirteen cells that were down there on that level.

What the hell was Chris playing at? This was not the time to be joking around! Satisfied that no-one was down there he returned to the girls in cell three. "Can't find him", he stated coldly.

"Well, check the other floors then, why don't you?" answered Beth annoyed as she was still consoling her friend in her arms.

"Yeah, sure- I'll get right on it boss", returned Lee sarcastically before heading back towards the stairs.

"Lee, there's no need for your sarcasm!" Beth shouted after him but he did not reply. Then she heard him mutter *stupid bitches* under his breath, as he opened the basement door with a grating creaking noise and was soon gone.

After he had left Beth concentrated on the needs of her friend. "How are you feeling Sam? Look, it's not your fault. I'm sure Chris will turn up somewhere... He's just playing a prank on you; that's all."

"No-one likes me", sobbed Sam through her muffled tears.

"Hey, that's not true- I like you a lot and so does Megan. Forget about the guys- they're a bunch of idiots and jerks let's face it", Beth replied consolingly.

"You think so? You're not just saying that are you? I didn't think Megan liked me very much either", Sam replied hopefully through her tears.

"Yes, she does... she likes you a lot and so do I. So don't be stupid and show these guys that you are tougher than they think you are and stand up to them if they're abusive towards you", Beth advised.

"You really think so?" Sam answered almost desperately.

"Yes, I do. So c'mon girl pull yourself together as we've got an investigation to do, okay?" Beth surmised.

Meanwhile, Lee was checking over the ground floor. Stopping suddenly he listened as he thought he'd heard something, some kind of sound but indistinct and distant. Moments passed and there was nothing further, so he shrugged and checked his watch: ten minutes to midnight; they had been there for just under two hours now. *One thing was for sure- at this rate it was going to be a long night. Also, where the hell was Chris and what was he playing at? After all, it was his idea that they come here in the first place!*
After his quick inspection of the ground floor that yielded nothing he headed upstairs back to Charlie on the first floor. Pausing momentarily at the stairwell door, he suddenly changed his mind. *Why go back to Charlie when fit Megan was waiting all alone on the second level?* Thus, decision made, he headed upwards.

Megan was fiddling with her long brown hair which she always wore loose rather than tied back as she preferred it that way. It felt freer somehow and more natural to her. She knew that she was pretty, as she spent a lot of time grooming and regarding her reflection in the mirror. It reinforced her sometimes fragile confidence in herself. Just then, Lee entered the room and approached her.
"Hi Megan, what's up?" he said.
"Yeah, fine Lee. Any sign of Chris? Is everything okay down there?" she replied.
He paused slightly as he came over and sat down next to her before answering in a more considerate manner, "It's just Sam's got all upset as Chris has disappeared on some prank that's all. Strangely, though I can't find him anywhere and it's not the kind of thing he normally does, is it? I mean when it comes to all-night ghost hunting vigils, he's normally deadly serious, besides the odd bit of messing around", Lee mused.

"Maybe it's because its Sam's first time with the group that he's trying to wind her up or something", Megan suggested.
"Yeah, could be... How are you doing anyway Megan? It seems quite a while since we had the chance to have a one-to-one chat."
"I'm fine... yeah I guess it is- is there anything in particular you wanted to talk about?" Megan inquired.
Lee pondered the situation thinking *that's a testing question, kind of provoking me to reveal my feelings towards her but at the same time she might just be having me on and not interested in the slightest. What do I say to that? Better play it cool,* he surmised as he continued, "Not really, it's just I really like talking to you, that's all."
Oh no, thought Megan, *he's trying a pick-up line* on me. She regarded him briefly before replying: blond shaven head, stockily built with incongruous facial features... *yep he really was definitely not her type! How do I reply? Best change the subject:* "What are we going to do about Chris?" she inquired.
"Oh, don't worry he'll turn up when he's tired of playing his silly little game, no doubt", answered Lee.
Megan felt really awkward as though he might make a move on her at any moment and quickly suggested, "Hey Lee, do you mind holding the fort here, while I go and check on Sam?"
"Sure, no problem Megan, go ahead", he replied ingratiatingly.
Relieved at his reply, Megan smiled and hurriedly got up and headed downstairs before he could change his mind.

Meanwhile, Charlie was getting bored on the first floor on his own. He wasn't getting any readings whatsoever on his monitoring equipment and it looked like he was going to be spending another

wasted evening waiting for spooks that never seemed to show up. Absentmindedly, he picked up the radio and inquired: "Hey guys, is everything okay down there? Have you found Chris yet? Get back to me, over."
Within moments Beth responded, as she really liked him as he was so good-looking, and had been secretly hoping he'd pay more attention to her: "Hey Charlie, yeah everything's fine down here, Sam just got a bit upset when Chris went missing, but Lee's gone to look for him, so hopefully he'll turn up soon."
"Is there anything I can do?" he asked.
Beth was unsure of how to reply, but she wanted to see him so she responded, "You could come down and help me- that would be great."
"With what?" he inquired nonchalantly.
"Oh, you know just to help calm things down around here", Beth replied feeling stupid.
Charlie paused slightly before shrugging his shoulders and answering, "Sure no problem Beth, see you in a minute."
Just as he was getting up Megan appeared. "Hey Charlie, I was just going downstairs to check on Sam."
"Hey Meg, yeah Beth just asked me to go down too. Might as well head down there together then", he finished matter-of-factly.
"Okay Charlie cool", she replied with an affectionate smile. Megan just wished he wasn't so laid back as she had been hoping that he would make a move on her for weeks now and she was almost contemplating jumping on him, especially if he kept her waiting much longer.

Sam had finally calmed down somewhat due to Beth's constant reassurance and had finally stopped crying. She was currently seated on the chair taking deep heavy breaths in an effort to quell her fears. Beth was in the process of checking the equipment they had down there and was looking at the various monitors and visual display screens with a bemused frown on her face. "We're getting some very strange readings", she said adding, "Never seen anything like it before- everything's totally off-the-scale... This can't be right- we must have some kind of glitch as nothing's working the way it's supposed to", she finished confused. Sam didn't respond as Beth continued to fiddle with the various dials and knobs of the various monitoring equipment whilst muttering to herself, *this is so weird!*

Just then Megan and Charlie joined them in the cell. "Hey Beth, how's it going?" inquired Charlie whilst Megan went over to console Sam.

"Not good", she replied, "We're getting all kinds of strange readings that don't make any sense. We must have some kind of malfunction or something", she finished dumbfoundedly.

"Okay, let me take a look", he replied joining her. After, a few minutes of checking the various monitors and sensors Charlie began to feel nearly as confused as Beth was. *Clearly, something was not right but what?*

Shortly afterwards Megan came over to them placing a hand tentatively on Charlie's shoulder, as she pretended to be engrossed in the various readouts from their equipment that, in truth, meant nothing to her even when they were supposedly functioning correctly. Suddenly, Sam shrieked a loud piecing scream of fear and horror which reverberated around the small confines of the cell with incredible volume. The other three almost jumped out of their skins, as they quickly turned to look at her, and to their mutual dismay, saw that she was covered from head to toe in blood, gore and what looked like fragments of body parts.

Within moments, Beth and Megan were screaming too in abject fear and horror. Charlie was so shocked and disgusted he felt like he was going to throw up any second now. Then he noticed that the flattened corpse and crushed skull that lay on top of Sam had broken, circular framed glasses just like Chris had been wearing that night, and the bits of clothing that still remained untarnished, matched what he had been dressed in. Uncontrollably, Charlie vomited where he stood and sprayed the nearby floor with a lumpy vile puke.

Meanwhile, the three girls were all still shrieking at the tops of their voices in utter panic and dismay; Sam was desperately trying to wipe Chris' remains from her but with some difficulty as she was totally covered with gore. Beth and Megan were alternately choking, screaming or gagging at the horrific sight. They too had not failed to notice the broken glasses stuck to the side of Sam's fat face which were covered in bits of brain and skull in a sickening sight. Also, that almost all of her rotund body and jumpsuit were covered in blood.

3.

Police officer Lauren Mitchell had stayed on late after her shift reviewing the old Anderson case files, more out of curiosity than anything else. Also, ever since they had discovered the bodies at Willowbrook, she had had an uneasy feeling about the place. She sensed somehow that there was something missing just like a lost jigsaw piece. Kristen had offered to help her but she had declined gratefully, and reluctantly, her partner had gone home.

The case had been filed away due to lack of evidence and no realistic leads to explore. The file contained numerous documents and notes from various detectives who had worked on the case and a lot of question marks. No-one who had seen the file had been able to make any sense of it so the conclusion had been that police time would be better spent elsewhere. As she made a cursory quick look through the various pages, she realised there was quite a lot to get through and it was already late. Without thinking, she placed the file in her holdall and headed home.

Later, nursing a large glass of red wine, she perused the file and spread out various documents in front of her on the coffee table. Lauren had changed out of her uniform and into a simple tracksuit which she felt most comfortable in and let her long blond hair down from the constrains of its bob. A frown sullied somewhat her pretty features, as she tried to make sense of the inexplicable happenings both at Willowbrook and the Anderson home.

It appeared that three detectives who had worked on the Anderson case had died during the investigation: Briggs, Noble and King. Also, John and Jess Anderson as well as their friends Sarah Hurd and her boyfriend Rick Clay, were too now deceased. The crime scene photographs were horrific to say the least. The bodies of inspector Briggs and John Anderson had been discovered in the dining room near to the chair which John had apparently removed from Willowbrook. She could make out what appeared to be a pentagram with various symbols she didn't recognise beneath it.

It seemed as though they were practising some kind of black magic ritual by the look of it. However, both their corpses looked like they had been mauled by a large wild animal such were the extent of their injuries which made no sense at all. She and Kristen had discovered the bodies of Jess, Sarah and the caretaker Paul Dickens in the basement at Willowbrook and the chair had clearly been brought back there *but why?* The latter had clearly had his throat cut from ear-to-ear but unfortunately the post-mortem on Sarah and Jess had proved inconclusive as to the cause of death.

Lauren then looked at the photo of King who clearly too had had his throat slit, so there was a connection there. Noble, however, looked like he had been beaten to death and his post-mortem had confirmed that a blunt, possibly wooden instrument as the murder weapon. That didn't really tie in at all. Finally, she grimaced as she looked at the pictures of Sarah's boyfriend Rick who had died of multiple first-degree burns which was even stranger. Sipping her wine she mulled over the transcripts of the recorded interviews to see if they may shed some light on the matter.

After a few pages, Lauren felt even more confused. It appeared that they had performed some kind of black magic ritual on the chair and, according to their accounts, had managed to travel to different dimensions in time. These *trips* as they termed them varied in length, some a matter of a few hours others up to twelve hours or more. Also, they believed that these *trips* were, in actual fact, the past memories of the former residents of Willowbrook who had died during procedures of electro-shock therapy.

Unwittingly, Lauren soon became engrossed in the documents spurred on by a perverse curiosity into the macabre. As she scrutinised page-by-page she made notes as she went along and before she knew it morning had come. Feeling pleased with herself, she then ordered her notes into a more coherent manner. Coincidentally, eleven people had died in the fire that had engulfed Willowbrook over twenty years ago and also eleven people had passed away during their procedures of electro-shock therapy via the chair. She formulated a list of the latter which read as follows:-

1. Harold Webb – a prolific paedophile and rapist – Jess' first trip described him trying to attack her.

2. Arthur Cooper – a member of the Order of Val Kyrie (weird cult) who was implicated in the murders of the Chesterfield family – In John's first trip he visits an old stately home and sees the corpses of Reginald and Jemima Chesterfield and their two daughters Elizabeth and Mary and their only son Jack.

3. Elizabeth Shaw

4. John Carey

5. Max Clifford

- John and Sarah described their trip together and how they were involved in a 50s robbery with those above- all three above went on to more serious crimes and eventually ended up in Willowbrook through pleading insanity.

6. Stephen Parkins- an ex-RAF fighter pilot during WWII – suffered 80% first degree burns when he was shot down and ended up in Willowbrook due to his deteriorating mental condition- link with Rick Clay's death

7. Alan Parker- murdered his wife and lover by bludgeoning them to death with a baseball bat and claimed insanity and ended up in Willowbrook – link with detective Noble's death

8. Andrew Murray- leader of the Order of Val Kyrie – witnessed murdering a young female by Jess and Sarah on their trip- they describe the murder weapon as a dagger with an ornate carved handle consisting off three embossed intertwining snakes set with emeralds- also he wore a ring with this same emblem.

9. William Cox

10. Rupert Williams

- Both the above spent over ten years together living in Africa and suffered nervous breakdowns after losing numerous members of their party whilst on safari – link to John Anderson's and inspector Briggs' deaths

11. Alan Pratt – no information

Not bad at all, she thought for a night's work. The only trouble was none of the above made much sense unless you actually believed that this chair could magically take you to another dimension in time and the memories of the former residents who'd died on it. Clearly, the whole idea was ludicrous and ridiculous; no wonder every detective who had worked on the case had wanted to shelve it as soon as possible. It was the kind of case that ended careers. Lauren yawned and headed off to bed, *I'll give it more thought tomorrow*, she promised herself.

Lee was busying himself fiddling with the various dials and buttons of their electronic equipment whilst he waited for Megan to return. He checked

his watch and it was just after 1am. He zipped up his jacket as it was suddenly feeling really cold up there. *All the readouts were off the scale –they just didn't make sense- maybe there was some magnetic interference or something?*
Just then a crunching noise originating from a far dark corner of the room distracted him. Megan and Beth had set up the equipment in the centre of what was originally or most probably a ward, as numerous charred bed-frames and mattresses lined both of the long side walls. He waited listening but could hear nothing more. Then, when he was about to return to the devices, he heard what sounded like heavy breathing distinctly closer sounding than before. Afraid, he got up and looked around pointing his flashlight in every far corner but nothing materialised.
Maybe it's Chris, he thought, *just messing about- it was about time he turned up, after all.* "Chris?" he said aloud but no answer came. *Shit!* He was beginning to feel very uneasy up there on his own in the dark with only the dim light from a few portable lamps for company. Somehow, he felt the urge to flee from the place without even bothering to say goodbye to anyone as his heart was now pounding violently in his chest and he was struggling to catch his breath. Lee quickly got out his asthma inhaler, that he liked to keep secret from the others, and squirted the fine spray into his mouth almost having a panic attack. Whilst he was doing so, he was almost oblivious to his surroundings as he was wheezing and choking for breath, but luckily, after a short while, the chemical took effect and he calmed down taking deep slow inhalations.
Unfortunately, the black demonic creature had taken this opportunity to approach him and now stood squarely right behind him. In one of its claws it held what looked like a broken metallic piece of a bed-frame which was pointed at one end. Lee

coughed, gurgling blood as the weapon was thrust through the back of his neck and revealed itself blood crimson in front of his face. Luckily, for Lee he did not last much longer, and felt forward towards the floor dead but the metallic shard held him up on one end, above the floor.
The creature growled and seemingly dissatisfied with its efforts it trudged off to the nearest bed-frame; the large claws on its feet grating on the stone floor as it walked. With great strength, it easily broke apart the corroded frame into four pieces. These it used to nail Lee to the wall, hanging him upside down in an inverted cross position. The demon grunted contentedly and left heading for the shadows.

Meanwhile, down in the basement everyone was in total panic and disarray. Sam had fallen to the floor desperately trying to wipe some of the blood and gore from her face whilst Charlie was still retching in a corner having thrown up many times already. Beth and Megan were crying disconsolately hugging one another, as though they were wishing this current nightmare would go away.

Finally, Charlie spluttered, "Let's get the hell out of here now!" He started towards the door in an attempt to flee from the interminable sight *that was now showing in cell 3 folks! You don't want to miss it! Get your tickets here!*
Beth and Megan watched him, through their clouded tear-stained vision, stumble towards the exit and they indecisively started to follow him. However, both of them could not help but pause and wonder whether to help Sam, who was still struggling on the floor, totally covered in gore and blood. Moments later they were both heading out of the cell guiltily, consoling themselves with the

thought *that they totally intended to go get help and come back to her as soon as they could, later!.*

Sam thought she was in hell. There she was totally covered from head to toe in blood and guts, most likely of Chris, and her two *so-called* best friends had deserted her. *Pull yourself together girl! You're stronger than this and have been through a lot worse!* Taking deep breaths, she attempted to rise to her feet with renewed vigour. Unfortunately, she slipped on the vast pool of blood in front of her and fell back into the chair. Moments later, she disappeared.

Sam awoke, after what had seemed like a rushing dream where she was rapidly spinning and twisting through a vortex and a blinding white tunnel to find that she was asleep in bed. Pretty soon afterwards self-consciously, she realised that she was in another person's mind. Suddenly, the droning beside alarm clock went off reading 7.30am. *Oh my God, Sam suddenly realised: I've got a penis!* She suddenly felt this man reach for his genitals and tug on his still flaccid member. Then he groaned as he looked at the time and Sam felt curiously unsatisfied when he left it alone. He stretched his arms out and got up and headed straight for the shower.
Again, Sam felt self-conscious and embarrassed when he reached for his member but the man seemed nervous about the time and decided against playing with his manhood. He quickly washed himself and got dressed and before Sam knew it, he was heading for work. *I wander what he does for a living?* She thought as she watched him driving to work. Sam didn't recognise where she was but the general landscape and surroundings, meant that he was clearly living in the suburbs of a city.

Finally later on, she got her answer: *it appeared that he was working in an office as an accountant*! Then pretty soon afterwards, she wished that he wasn't, as Sam found herself watching him spend hour after hour looking in books and checking figures on computer spreadsheets, as well as adding up sums on his pocket calculator. Occasionally, he'd speak to one of his colleagues in a nearby booth, or get up to go to the toilet or get a drink, but most of the time, just sitting there at h is desk calculating. *Boredom City!* Sam thought frustratingly.

Occasionally, the man's superior came by and told him off, sometimes angrily and others times more placatingly. He seemed to be doing a lot wrong, no question, but Sam couldn't help but wince a bit when she realised how much he was sucking up to his boss. *Taking a load of shit, yet eating it and at the same time doing nothing!* She even wished she was somewhere else, *anywhere but here.*

The hours went by slowly but surely interminably and even Sam felt herself watching the clock every time this man had it in view. Finally, after a laborious day, it was suddenly all over, and he got up, left the office and headed to his car in the parking lot. After he got in, he drove back to the suburbs and finally, after a short drive, arrived home. As he seemed to have no live-in wife or girlfriend, he was greeted by no-one. No pets either, by the look of it, to give him loving warmth and affection.

He turned on the TV and watched some inane program requiring the mental faculties of an adolescent for hours in between fixing dinner. Then, he checked his watch, and went to the bathroom. As he looked into the mirror, Sam could finally take a look at his reflection: he was average looking with short cut dark hair and a pleasant looking smile. The man grinned at his reflection, whilst squirting

deodorant under his arms. Sam thought, *he's quite good-looking but nothing special but clearly, he thinks he's a lot more handsome than he is- type.*
The man ate a disgusting TV dinner whilst watching the TV. Then, he spoke to someone on the phone and arranged to go out that evening, and Sam discovered it was his friend Rob who called him Alan whilst talking. *So, I know his name at least,* she thought. Later, after checking his hair in the mirror and changing his clothes, he heads out into a moonlit night. Hailing a taxi, he gets in and hums to himself whilst checking his mobile phone. He looks at a few texts and then smiles to himself and furiously moves both thumbs and forefingers as he types in a reply.
The taxi arrives at some bar, and he goes in and after walking around for a bit, he discovers his friends all parked up in a corner. Joining them, after the initial greeting, the man gets in the drinks. Sam watches him and his friends drink, drink after drink until they all seem nearly paralytic. They even play various drinking games all sat around a wooden table. Now and then, they order shots from the bar. Finally, they decide to leave and go to a nightclub.
Alan tries it on with everything that moves in the club, whilst occasionally venturing onto the dance-floor with a drink in his hand and shaking his hips in a strange type of jive, to a unique if odd rhythm. Sam laughs at the pathetic pick-up lines he tries out to no avail. Also, none of his friends seem to fair much better. Then they all head for the bar and drink numerous pints of beer and shorts. Later, Sam sees him crouched over the *throne*, throwing-up in the toilet. *The TV dinner certainly came up, that's for sure,* she thought.
Finally, Alan heads home in a taxi on his own. He staggers to get his key in the door before stumbling up the stairs, quickly undressing and then passing

out on the bed. Sam wondered *how long this was going to go on for. Hopefully, not for too much longer as it was far too depressing. How had this happened to her in the first place?*

The next morning, the man was rushing down the stairs of the subway to catch the train for work. He was late and nursing a very bad hangover. Sam felt every bit as sick as he did, sharing his suffering and the misery that he felt. For some reason, he decided to wait at the very edge of the platform. The next train to pass through the station was not scheduled to stop. Within a few minutes, the rumble of the approaching train could be felt echoing about the confined space.

To Sam's horror, the man jumped out in front it as it passed through the station. She felt a momentary flash of intense pain and then complete nothingness as she drifted away. His act caused pandemonium in the station with people screaming, crying and even throwing up at the sight of the macabre spectacle. Alan's body was ripped apart and he was decapitated with much blood and gore splattering everywhere. His head went spinning off to the side and rolled down the tunnel, to somewhere out of sight.

Megan and Beth were doing their best to catch up with Charlie who was already half way up the stairs ahead of them, desperate in his intent to escape from the place. Finally he reached the ground level and tried to open the door which led out from the stairwell, but it wouldn't budge. As he was struggling, trying to pull the handle, he found that he had to put his flashlight on the floor nearby so that he could exert more force. The girls caught up with him.

"What's up?" asked Megan.

"The bloody door's locked and it won't open!" cried Charlie as he slammed his shoulder into it and then

tried several kicks but to no avail. The extra light from their flashlights meant at least he could see what he was doing. "How could it be locked? It was open earlier- I mean we're the only ones here, so who could have locked it?" he screamed in despair.
"Here let me try", said Beth.
"Be my guest!" Charlie replied angrily, slamming his palm against the nearby wall, "Fuck!" he finished.
Both girls tried to open the door but they had no luck either. "What are we going to do?" inquired Megan fearfully.
"How the fuck do I know!" Charlie screamed before calming himself somewhat and continuing, "Hold on a second... yeah maybe its Lee messing about- where the hell is he, anyway?"
"I left him on the second floor, keeping an eye on the equipment when I went to check on Sam", Megan responded querulously.
The darkness all around them seemed to be closing in somehow with only the weak beams given off by their pocket flashlights to illuminate the surroundings. The dark had become strangely thicker and almost tactile. A steady dripping noise, from somewhere nearby, echoed all around them, amplified by the silence.
"C'mon, let's check upstairs, see if we can find Lee", suggested Beth.
The others nodded agreement and they headed up the stairs to the top floor, occasionally stumbling on fallen debris as they made their ascent in the weak light. Reaching the second level, Charlie tried the door and, to his relief, it was open. Just as he opened the door though, a piercing inhuman shrieking noise filled the air and reverberated all around them. It appeared to be originating from somewhere below.
"Who the fuck was that?" cried Charlie. The girls didn't respond as they were petrified and standing still unmoving like rabbits caught in lamplight.

Then they clearly heard crunching noises on the fallen debris that littered the stairwell below. It seemed that whoever it was, they were coming up. Still holding the door ajar, Charlie shouted, "C'mon get the fuck inside!" and roughly pushed the girls through the open doorway.

Recovering slightly from their trancelike state of abject fear, they awkwardly managed to get their legs moving and stumble inside with Charlie following close behind them.

"Try and find something we can use to block the door shut", Charlie demanded frantically, holding it closed and bracing his body against it. The girls looked around the large ward for something of use. Unfortunately, as their lights darted about the room, the beam of Megan's flashlight happened to reveal Lee nailed upside down on the wall; his clothing covered in his blood. She screamed and screamed in resolute and absolute horror and despair.

Beth ran towards her friend and too caught sight of Lee pinned to the wall like a rag doll, his dull lifeless eyes seemed to be staring right back at them. She cried out in horror and utter misery and instantly began weeping inconsolably. Soon the two girlfriends were hugging each other and crying hysterically in each others arms. Charlie was in two minds- he needed to man the door but also he wanted to see what the hell had upset them so much.

Joining the girls he quickly realised and cried out, "Holy fuck! We need to get the hell out of here!" Leaving the girls entwined together, he quickly scanned the room for something he could use as a weapon to defend himself. Unfortunately, there was hardly anything of use or so it seemed- just charred, rusted bed-frames and rotted mattresses. He thought of trying to break one of former apart but then decided against, instead opting to grab one of the portable lamps, they'd brought with them that were on stands. It was not much, but better than nothing.

Charlie rushed back towards the door, just in case whoever it was that he'd heard previously, had managed to climb the rest of the stairs. Just as he reached the door, it swung open and he was confronted by what appeared to be a demonic entity- totally black and charred with burning red eyes which appeared to be on fire. Before, his conscious mind could totally comprehend the hideous vision in front of him he felt a searing and unimaginable pain as the creature thrust two of its large claws into his eye sockets. Charlie screamed in excruciating agony as the devilish being churned its long pointed nails around within his head.

Megan and Beth heard his cries but felt helpless to do anything, as fear and loathing had rooted them to the spot where they stood, entwined together crying and screaming uncontrollably. Soon Charlie was no longer audible, as the creature's long claws dug around inside his head. It dropped his body by the doorway and paused indecisively, looking towards the girls huddled closely together. The demon almost seemed to shrug its shoulders as it left to return downstairs; its claws scraping and echoing on the floor as it moved.

Police officers Lauren Mitchell and Kristen Gallagher were out on patrol on a, so far at least, quiet night-shift. Hardly any calls had come through from dispatch and they were just driving around aimlessly, looking for any potential criminal activity. Lauren hadn't mentioned yet, the research she had done on Willowbrook and the Anderson case the previous night but even so, that place was still on her mind. In actual fact, since they had first gone there, she had been thinking about it constantly; *call it a hunch or her sixth sense but something was clearly wrong about that place.*

"Hey Kristen, do you mind if we swing by Willowbrook and just check it's all secure, as I don't know why, but that place has been playing on my mind ever since we went there the other day."

"Yeah sure, it's a quiet enough night but, if a call comes in, we'll have to prioritise it", Kristen replied professionally.

Lauren wasted no time in getting there and soon they arrived. Kristen got out of the passenger door to check the gates. A stiff breeze whistled around her as she did so in that dark moonless night. *The chains were haphazardly in place and the lock had been clearly cut- they were open.* Kristen gathered up the chain by weaving it in and out of the bars and slung it on the ground, out of the way. Then she opened the gates and returned to the squad car.

"Something's up, the gates are open and the lock's been cut", Kristen said nonchalantly as she got back in. Lauren drove through the gates and headed to Willowbrook which stood just over the brow of the hill on the approach road. Five minutes later, Lauren parked alongside the van which was directly outside the main entrance. "We have company", she said as they both got out and removed their flashlights to check over the van. Kristen called the registration plate into despatch and a few minutes later they confirmed back to her that it belonged to a Chris Turner of so-and-so address, no previous convictions except a minor for trespass.

"Okay, let's check it out", said Lauren and the officers headed inside.

4.

Megan and Beth had finally managed to untwine themselves and had gone over to Charlie but his corpse had set their tirade of screaming and crying off again. After some while, they had managed to calm themselves down enough to separate and decide on a course of action; both still had tears in their eyes and were weeping intermittently but the need for self-preservation had taken control.

"What are we going to do?" asked Beth fearfully.

"I'm not sure- maybe we could check the first floor windows and see if we could get out that way", Megan suggested.

"But that creature is somewhere down there!" replied Beth worriedly.

"I know, but what choice do we have? If we stay here it might come back anyway", Megan stated matter-of-factly.

"Okay, let's try and do that", responded Beth nervously.

"We'll have to be as quiet as we can – if we see it we'll just have to run back up here… C'mon let's go before I lose my bottle", finished Megan.

The girls cautiously stepped down the two flights of stairs that led to the first level, carefully avoiding any fallen debris and moving slowly, their flashlights guiding their way; dim beams in the omniscient black. Reaching the first level, Megan tried the stairwell door and luckily it was open. They proceeded inside nervously, expecting the creature to appear at any time. They traversed a corridor and then entered the spacious open ward where Charlie and Lee had set up most of their equipment earlier.

Looking around, they sighed with relief as they appeared to be on their own. However, there were

still plenty of dark corners and places to hide as their flashlights illuminated very little. They moved over to the nearest window and looked out. The drop appeared to be about twenty feet; too far really to jump without risking serious injury or worse.
Then Megan noticed the patrol car parked up close to their van. "Thank God", she sighed, "The police are here!"
"I can't believe it", replied Beth, "They've actually turned up at a time when we really need them", she joked half-heartedly.
"Let's go down to the ground floor and bang on the door and let them know we're here, as maybe they can force it open", Megan suggested. Beth nodded eagerly and they headed back to the stairwell.

Meanwhile, Lauren and Kristen were doing a cursory search of the ground level with their flashlights held high above shoulder level and their free hands poised on the holsters of their revolvers, just in case. So far they had found nothing- all the rooms appeared to be empty. So they decided to check the other floors and headed for the stairwell following the overhead signs.
Just as they were approaching the door, they heard two girl's voices screaming for help and banging on it. Lauren and Kristen rushed towards the door. Lauren called through, "Who's there?"
Megan responded with Beth pleading too, "Help us please! There's someone after us and we can't get the door open!"
"Okay, calm down both of you", responded Kristen immediately trying the door- they were right, it was locked. Instinctively, Kristen withdrew her weapon and aimed it at the door. "Get back! I'm going to shoot the lock out –tell me when you're clear", she ordered. Pausing, she waited until their muffled acknowledgements that they were away from the vicinity of the door came through.

Kristen fired a few shots at the lock and then stopped to check to see if the door would give, but it still held. Just then she heard the girls inside screaming frantically, in abject horror and excruciating pain. Kristen quickly stepped back and fired successive rounds at the lock until finally it gave. She quickly opened the door and shone her flashlight around as did Lauren behind her, but there was no-one to be seen.

Megan and Beth had not noticed the creature approach them from behind and whilst the police officer had fired at the lock, it had grabbed them both by the back of the neck with its claws slightly penetrating their flesh. It had then held them both high in the air in front of it and quickly proceeded to jump down the two flights of stairs which led to the basement level. As Kristen and Lauren entered the stairwell upstairs, the demon had reached cell three and flung them both towards the chair in the far corner. They had landed in a heap on top of it with their legs and arms intermingled and had immediately disappeared.

Andrew Murray, the leader of the Order of Val Kyrie couldn't believe his luck when these two nubile females had materialised. Just the way he liked them- in their late teens or early twenties even though, he was in his late sixties. He liked to defile their innocence, that was the thing, and through worshipping his master Satan over the years, he had found such rewards popped up from time-to-time; these he merited to his continued faithful service.
He suddenly recalled the last two girls who had curiously appeared seemingly out of nowhere, during a previous sacrificial ceremony: the beautiful blond who he'd had taken to his chambers and the

pretty brunette whose throat he'd been about to cut when they had both miraculously disappeared. This time though, he was determined that wasn't going to happen again. So he wasted no time realising that he'd taken far too long that time before, and thus, allowed those two to get away.

Megan and Beth awoke, almost simultaneously, from what had seemed like an unimaginable rushing swirling vortex of iridescent light and strange sounds, to find that they were in a large cavernous room languishing on a chequered floor naked. All around them were dark figures cloaked in robes with hoods still up. Some sat on separate thrones and had gold embroidery on the front of their clothing, as though they maintained higher status in this weird group, whatever it was. They had been placed on the floor in front of their apparent leader who appeared to have a large erection which made his robe stick out at the front towards them.

Murray quickly decided that he preferred the brunette with the ponytail but, in truth, there was little to choose between them; they were both beautiful. His followers begin their rhythmical chanting as he unsheathed the antique dagger, which bore the emblem of their order: three intertwining snakes ornately carved into the handle and set with emeralds. Stepping forward, he swiped the dagger across Megan's throat and she slumped to the floor instantly dead with her lifeblood pouring out of her. Beth screamed hysterically on witnessing her friend being brutally murdered in front of her eyes.

Two guards then approached and dragged her off as she continued to cry out heartbrokenly. Murray followed close behind them, as they escorted her to his chambers. *This time he was not going to miss out on his prize.* Shortly afterwards, the guards threw her on the bed in his room and retired, bowing towards Murray as they left. He quickly removed his robe and placed the blood covered dagger carefully on a side-board. Then he quickly jumped on top of Beth, as she screamed once more and tried frantically to fight him off.

However, he was too strong for her and her weak blows only seemed to encourage him further. He clearly was enjoying her misery and suffering. With a satisfied grunt he penetrated her, at the same time pinning both her arms down on the bed. He thrust harder and harder until after a few minutes he couldn't contain himself any longer and ejaculated with an ecstatic cry. Murray quickly got off her, put his robe back on and left locking the door behind him leaving her tearfully moaning in self-pity. He grinned to himself as he paced down the passageway; he would come back and service her again, as soon as he felt able to do so.

Beth wept inconsolably hugging herself protectively for a short while before forcing herself to regain her senses and take control. *Whatever happened, she didn't want to feel that hideous old man's touch and wrinkled skin ever again.* Through her tear-stained vision she searched the room frantically. In a wardrobe she found a robe and she quickly put it on and covered herself. Then her eyes focused on the dagger; its blade a malevolent crimson on the sideboard. *In his haste, he must have forgotten it!* She rushed over and picked it up with some relief and wiped it on the bedcover. Anger arose within her as she cleaned her friend's blood off the blade. *If he dared to come back in here, she would have her revenge for the both of them.*

Lauren and Kristen had entered the stairwell and found it empty. They headed down into the pitch black of the basement with their flashlights and revolvers held out before them. They forced open the door and grimaced at the dank vile corrupt smell emanating from there, which they both remembered only too well. They had a cursory look in the first two cells which were again empty and moved on quickly to cell three.

They both gagged and retched simultaneously on stepping inside as the whole area in front of the chair was covered in blood, gore and body parts. Clearly, there were multiple fatalities. Kristen hurriedly took out her radio but she could get no reception so she rushed upstairs to call it in to headquarters. Lauren only just managed to stop herself throwing up and polluting the crime scene as her flashlight revealed a fat girl's head which had rolled into a corner.

Shortly afterwards, Kristen returned and notified her that they were sending every available unit ASAP. They quickly searched the other cells in the basement but found nothing. Next they checked the upper floors. In a first floor ward, they came across a lot of electronic monitoring equipment, portable lamps and censors but no-one was there. On the second floor they both grimaced in shock once more on seeing the young man pinned to the wall upside down with what appeared to be multiple metallic shards.

"What the hell is going on here?" ejaculated Kristen.

Lauren shrugged, "Beats me, we've walked into a scene from a horror movie- I mean the basement's like a bloodbath!"

"What I can't figure is that we both definitely heard two girl's voices through the ground level stairwell door and yet we've searched every room and they're nowhere to be found!" Kristen surmised confusion and incomprehension in her tone.

"I know. Where the hell did they go? We checked the windows- none seemed to have been opened in a long while- so where are they?" Lauren inquired bemused. Kristen nodded silently lost in thought, not really knowing what more to say. In quiet contemplation they headed back down to the ground floor to await their colleagues.

Within fifteen minutes, it seemed as though half the police department had turned up: multiple squad cars, forensics, numerous detectives, and the works. Lauren took some of their team to the second floor whilst Kristen guided the others to the basement. A rookie officer vomited as soon as he took a look into cell three and was chastised and sent back upstairs. No-one could make sense or understand what had taken place, especially in regard to the fact that it had only been a matter of months since the last horrific episode there. However, this one was clearly far worse by far.

Detectives from the homicide division again took control and once more Lauren and Kristen were pushed to the sidelines after giving their initial accounts. Forensics moved in and body parts were bagged and tagged and sent for analysis. Post-mortems were quickly scheduled and everyone involved knew that clearly they'd be working throughout the night. Later on, the blood and gore splattered chair was removed from the basement and brought up to the ground floor- this time it was going to be taken in for evidence.

It was nearly 5am and Lauren and Kristen had two more hours to go before they ended their shift. They headed back to the station in their patrol car to write up their reports as they both thought they'd seen just about enough for one night. By 6am, they had more-or-less finished doing their write-ups, when they saw the chair being brought back into the station by two burly officers. As it was too large an item for the evidence room, they placed it in interview room one for the time being. It had been wrapped in thin plastic to contain the forensic evidence and to prevent any leakage.

Beth waited for what seemed to be an interminable time behind the door of the leader's chambers, expectantly waiting for him to return. It had seemed like hours to her, but it was possibly only ten or fifteen minutes that had passed. Then finally, she heard the lock turn quietly in the door and the handle move downwards as it suddenly opened before her. Murray slipped in the room and quickly closed the door behind him. As he did so Beth slammed the dagger squarely into his chest with all the force that she could muster.

Murray would have screamed but blood gurgled in his mouth from his wound, and he was unable to do so- all he could manage was a choking pain filled croak, and then nothing as he fell to the floor dead. Satisfied, Beth stood over him victorious as revenge had clearly been served. Just as she was wandering what to do next she found curiously that she was beginning to dematerialise. Her body was becoming translucent and losing its vitality and essence. She watched in fascination as she disappeared gradually and then rushed once more into the swirling vortex of blinding white light.

It was just after 6am and both Lauren and Kristen had just finished writing their reports. Only an hour of their shift to go before home and much needed rest; they both thought silently. Lauren got up and headed towards interview room one and Kristen immediately sensing her intent, followed. They both entered the room and sat at the seats behind the desk and looked towards the malevolent chair.

"There's something very wrong with this chair", Lauren stated aggrieved.

"I know", agreed Kristen, "It gives me the creeps and how many deaths have we witnessed around it already- something, I'm not sure what, is definitely not right about it."

Lauren nodded knowingly and was just about to reply when two figures reappeared on top of the chair underneath the plastic wrapping. One was clearly dead, as it almost immediately fell forwards motionless but was constrained by the plastic. The other person suddenly began to frantically start punching and trying to tear their way out of the confines of the wrapping. It seemed as though the figure was struggling for breath and trying to fight their way to freedom.

Surprised and shocked simultaneously, Lauren and Kristen took a few seconds to react before Kristen quickly removed a pocket knife from her belt and cut through the thin plastic. A pretty, but dishevelled brunette was revealed who immediately gasped for breath, and inhaled deeply multiple times gratefully. When she had recovered sufficiently, Lauren and Kristen helped lift her out of the plastic confines and sat her down on one of the seats nearby. The other body immediately fell to the bottom of the wrapping. They could see it was a girl also, whose throat had been cut and her body was covered in her own blood.

The mysterious girl took a while to recover sufficiently enough to speak and Lauren tried to console her whilst Kristen got on the radio to inform homicide what had just happened. The inspector who answered her call became indignant thinking she must be joking about, *as what she was describing was just not possible!* However, due to her continued insistence, he agreed to send a pair of detectives back to the station to check it out. However, he also could not help himself but threaten to have her fired and take her badge if what she had stated turned out to be not the case.

“Where am I?” said Beth confused.

Suddenly, Lauren and Kristen both noticed that this girl held in her hands what appeared to be a bloody dagger! They quickly removed it from her

grasp and placed it into a plastic evidence bag which Kristen placed by her side whilst they began to question her. “You are with the police now so you’re safe... Who are you?” inquired Lauren.
The girl stuttered tearfully before responding, “I can’t believe they’re all dead!”
“What’s your name?” Lauren asked gingerly whilst Kristen took out a pad and began to make notes.
Distracted, the girl replied, “Beth... Beth Maloney.”
“So what happened to you tonight, Beth?” Lauren said softly. The girl did not respond as she was still crying fitfully. Patiently, Lauren asked, “Beth, I know it’s hard for you, but try to tell us what happened from the beginning.”
“I’m part of a group that investigates paranormal activity”, Beth responded quietly. “We sometimes do work for a small cable channel... A few months ago, Chris our leader, told us about some strange goings on at the old Willowbrook mental institution that he had seen reported mainly on the internet but also through other media...”
“Lauren, can I have a quick word outside?” interrupted Kristen.
Lauren nodded, “Okay Beth, we’re just going outside the room for a minute but do your best to think back, so you can describe to us what happened, okay?” Beth nodded and the two partners reassembled in the corridor.
“Lauren, we can’t proceed with this interview- we’re not detectives and it could jeopardise their lines of investigation... Also, if we mess up we could both lose our badges...” Kristen stated matter-of-factly.
“I know but aren’t you even curious to ask this girl what’s been going on? I’m just trying to make some sense of it, that’s all and, at this minute, she appears to have all the answers”, Lauren responded curtly.
“Just watch yourself partner, that’s all I’m saying”, replied Kristen.

"Okay fine, just a couple more questions, okay?" Lauren answered decisively. Kristen nodded her approval silently and they headed back into the room.

Lauren sat back down beside Beth and carefully prompted her to continue her story. The girl looked at her sheepishly before replying, "So last night we got our small group together and headed down to Willowbrook around 10pm. We split up in pairs: Chris and Sam headed down to the basement whilst Lee and Charlie took the first floor and Megan and I, the second... We all set up our equipment and kept it touch via our radios... A few hours into our vigil, Sam informed us that Chris had gone missing..."

"Lauren", Kristen interrupted once more, "That's enough; otherwise we'll get in serious trouble." Her partner paused indecisively, desperate to find out more from their only source of information but finally acquiesced and they both left Beth behind in the room.

"Well, I suppose at least we found out something", Lauren replied disappointedly.

Just then two recognisable homicide detectives turned up and headed towards them- Lucas and Chohan.

Kristen spoke up as they stood together outside interview room one: "Two girls just magically appeared on that weird fucking chair right before our very eyes so before you say anything- realise we don't have a clue how it happened- it just did... one's dead, one's alive."

Chohan replied indignantly, "Look, we're going to need your statements."

Kristen answered curtly, "You'll get them tomorrow, we're both going home- it's been a very long night", she finished shoving the plastic evidence bag containing the blood-stained dagger towards them. Lucas and Chohan were about to object but the two female officers had already headed off and they just shrugged at each other and went inside the interview room, hopefully to get some answers.

Later, Megan's body had been removed but the chair had been left where it was even though there was now a slight stain beneath it on the thin carpet. Lucas and Chohan now joined Beth to start the formalised, taped first interview session. She had tearfully responded to their questions and recounted all that night's events to the two detectives who listened in a mixture of shock, awe and wonder. They cross-examined her forcibly but she still came up with the same answers. She gave the names of all the victims but only knew a few of their addresses.

After Beth's initial account, Lucas and Chohan met outside the room to confer, as nothing she had told them made any sense whatsoever. The mutilated bodies of the victims though could not be argued with. The weird robe or cloak that she was wearing was confiscated and sent to the lab for analysis after a female officer of similar size had leant her some casual clothes to wear for the time being.

However, her story seemed to consist of more fantasy than reality. Also, she had supposedly reappeared with the dead girl Megan, who had seemingly died from a single throat laceration, with Beth holding a blood-stained dagger in her hands. The detectives couldn't help but assume the obvious- that she was most likely, the culprit. They sent the dagger immediately to forensics and awaited the results.

"I wish I wasn't on this case", said Lucas sadly.

"I know man, me too", replied Chohan, "We'll just have to see what forensics comes up with- I really don't know what to say, this is like working on some *X-files* kind of shit and, the last I heard, we don't have a *Mulder or Scully* in the department."

Both muttering obscenities, they returned to their desks, leaving Beth locked-up in the interview room. "At least she gave us the full names and some addresses of the victims which can be confirmed with forensics", Lucas stated hopefully.
"Yeah true- it's just her account of their deaths, doesn't make any sense at all", added Chohan, "I mean she described some kind of demonic creature as being the perpetrator of some of them. Conveniently, for her, she doesn't know how the others died except for her friend Megan who had her throat slit right in front of her by some weird cult member who then raped her afterwards. She then supposedly dematerialises back on the chair with her friend whilst clutching the probable murder weapon..."
"Yeah I know, you couldn't write this shit, it's so fucked up!" Lucas jeered.
"I mean did you see the state of some of those bodies down in that damn basement?" Chohan added incredulously. "It looked like the Texas chain-saw massacre down there- body parts, blood and gore everywhere..." he finished trailing off, lost in thought.
"Well until we get that forensics report, there's not much more that we can do here- let's get that girl locked up in a cell for the night... You know she looks pretty fit to me- if she wasn't so messed up and dishevelled", responded Lucas.
"I'd give her one, definitely any day", replied Chohan.
"Yeah, me too- no question... Pity about her mind though, it's clearly all fucked-up!" Lucas answered grinning at his partner.
The detectives arranged for Beth to be accommodated in a cell for the night for further questioning tomorrow and after filing their reports, they headed off to their separate homes. On both their journeys strangely, both Lucas and Chohan

were thinking the same thing unbeknownst to each other: firstly, *this is the weirdest case I've ever worked on*; secondly, *none of the evidence or very little makes sense* and thirdly, *how do I get off this bullshit case which is, more than likely, going to end my career?*

5.

At Willowbrook, the police department worked alongside forensics and the coroner, throughout the night, removing the bodies and taking a multitude of samples. A new lock was fitted to the front doors as they didn't want anyone else getting in so easily and thus, hopefully there would be no more casualties. Also, a squad car was positioned at the gates, which had been securely locked and chained, and maintained on a 24/7 basis; one shift replacing another in turn, to prevent any further mishaps.

Lauren and Kristen both arrived at the station for their late afternoon shift to find that Beth was once again being questioned by detectives Lucas and Chohan in interview room one; the chair an ominous presence in the background. As Lauren looked through the one-way observing window, she noticed that the chair seemed to have been cleaned as there was no longer any blood or gore on it. All she could see was a slight stain below it on the carpet. *Why would they do that? It seemed odd that they would remove such evidence!*

Inside the room the two detectives were looking dumbfoundedly at Beth as she recounted her version of events. Earlier that morning, a female doctor had come by to examine her and take various swab samples from her vagina due to her alleged claim of a recent rape. Such an allegation had to be taken seriously, however unlikely it may have been. After which, Beth had been allowed to take a shower and change into a simple blouse and blue jeans that had been lent to her. Then she had been taken to the interview room for further questioning.

Lucas stared at the attractive young woman in front of him as she came to the end of her account. It had taken some while, as she had often stopped and broken into tears, especially when recalling some of the horrific events that, according to her, had taken place that night. When she had finished, he scratched his shaven head and pondered silently for a moment- *he had served in the force for nearly twenty years now and thought he had heard it all, but clearly he had not!* He was now in his mid-forties, his short hair showing signs of grey which framed his gaunt and hardened features.

Lucas looked over at Chohan who was a similar age to him but of Asian descent with a tough imposing expression that he seemed to wear at all times. His partner nodded at him to begin, as he was taking the lead on this one. During her account they had both sat there quietly taking notes, but now was the time to try and pick holes in her story and see if it held up to a lengthy examination. Lucas stood up and looked at Beth squarely in the eye and began a makeshift summary of her version of events.

"Okay, correct me if I'm wrong", he began his tone almost condescending, "You arrived at Willowbrook around 10pm last night in a van registered to a Chris Turner who was also present along with a Lee Chiles, Megan Cliff, Charlie Baker and a Sam Matheson. Charlie cut the chains and the lock at the main gates and you parked up outside the entrance..." Lucas finished glancing at Beth who just nodded.

"You are all part of a group that investigates the paranormal and occasionally does work for a small cable channel... You entered Willowbrook shortly after 10pm and split up into three groups to set up your equipment: Chris and Sam took the basement; Charlie and Lee the first floor and you and Megan the first. The plan was to do an all night vigil at the premises... You're not that clear on the timings but you think probably an hour or so later, Sam called up on the radio to say that Chris had gone missing", Lucas paused again for her corroboration which she gave again with a nod.

Lucas continued, "So you and Lee go down to check on her and search for Chris, who you both think must be playing a prank... Then you comfort Sam whilst Lee goes to check the other floors and ends up with Megan on the second. Again you're not sure of the timings but maybe a half hour later, you call Charlie and ask him to come down to help you with Sam... Shortly afterwards, Megan too joins you downstairs, stating that she had just left Lee on the second floor. Sam sits on the chair and suddenly gets covered with the flattened and mutilated body parts of Chris...

You Charlie and Megan then proceed to leave Sam to get help and find that the ground floor stairwell door is locked. You check the upstairs floors for a way out and come across the body of Lee nailed to the wall..." Lucas paused as Beth had, once again, started weeping. Ignoring her he continued, "Charlie is then killed by some demonic-like creature with red eyes that you only glimpsed briefly, by the second floor doorway. You and Megan then check the first floor and see a police patrol car outside. You bang on the ground floor door and cry out to the officers..." Lucas again paused measuring the effect of his words on her.

"The officers try to shoot the lock out but this demonic creature appears once more and grabs you and takes you down to the basement and throws you both onto the chair causing you to dematerialise and reappear in some kind of underground cavern where a strange cult ritual is taking place... Your clothes have been removed and Megan is immediately murdered with some ornate dagger by the cult leader who has you dragged off to his private quarters by two guards. He then

proceeds to rape you and shortly afterwards, leave the room. When he returns later you stab him with this same dagger- the one you were found holding last night in this very room", he finished accusingly.
"That's right", Beth stuttered through her tear-stained vision.
Lucas couldn't hide his distain as he replied, "Are you a writer? I'll buy that- hey maybe you should send your script to Sam Raimi, sounds like he's about the only person who could do something with it! You really expect us to believe that?" He stormed at her as he left the room before she could reply with Chohan following closely behind him.
"Can you believe her shit?" Lucas fumed.
His partner replied calmly, "No, certainly not all of it but there's probably specs of truth buried beneath what she's saying- that's our job isn't it- to find out what they are."
Chohan's cool demeanour helped to placate Lucas somewhat and he nodded back taking a few deep breaths as he did so. Just then a forensics officer came along and handed over the lab report on the dagger. Lucas took the file and opened it with interest- perhaps some desperately needed answers were inside. Two types of blood had been found on it- one a positive match for Megan and the other had been identified as a former resident of Willowbrook, an Andrew Murray who had died there whilst being administered electro-shock therapy. He was a known member of some weird religious cult called the *Order of Val Kyrie*.
Lucas stared incomprehensively into space, his mind desperately trying to decipher what he had just read. "I think we've just entered the *Twilight Zone*", he finally said handing Chohan the report. His partner looked at it too in utter bewilderment.
"C'mon I need a drink", finished Lucas heading towards the door. Chohan just shrugged and followed taking the file with him.

Shortly afterwards in a bar across the street, they were drinking beers with whiskey chasers. They downed the shots in one at the bar and took the beers over to a corner table. "How is it possible?" said Chohan bemused, "I mean this Andrew Murray must have died over twenty years ago before the fire that engulfed the place- so how can his blood be on the murder weapon?"
"I know, you tell me, *I just work here*", Lucas replied.
"That's not to mention the robe she was wearing when she appeared- what if it too has his DNA on it?" added Chohan speculatively.
His partner looked back at him in agreement, "This reminds me of what Tom Hanks said in that film, 'Saving Private Ryan.' What did he say? You know when Ryan refuses to go with him? Yeah, something like, *this has just taken a turn for... the surreal* or some shit like that. That's exactly how I'm feeling."

Later, the detectives went to get a couple of burgers to neutralise the effects of the alcohol and after quickly consuming them, they headed back to the station. Shortly afterwards, they got the report back on the cloak and yes, it was a positive DNA match to Andrew Murray, deceased. *This just keeps getting better and better*, Lucas thought sarcastically. Also, all the corpses, body parts and general gore had been matched with Beth's five accomplices to the break-in at Willowbrook.
Their respective parents were now currently being informed. Beth's parents too had been notified but were told that for the next forty-eight hours, she could have no visitors whatsoever; they would have to wait. Post-mortems had been carried out on the victims; unnecessarily perhaps in the case of Lee, Megan and Charlie as their wounds clearly indicated the manner of their deaths. The various body parts of Sam that had been recovered were

consistent with those suffered in road accidents or train suicides. The little left of Chris' pulverised remains were inconclusive but consistent with being run-over by a truck or other heavy moving object.

The detectives had Beth taken back to her holding cell as they really had no more to ask her for the time being; they needed to do some digging on what evidence they had first. She was glad to be removed from the interview room as the chair's presence was frightening, especially to one who had experienced its power. Chohan took a look at the Anderson case files (which Lauren had since replaced) and Lucas concentrated his efforts on finding out more about Willowbrook and the deaths that had occurred there with particular emphasis on Murray and his cult, the *Order of Val Kyrie*.

Lauren and Kristen returned to the department shortly after 12pm after a tiring afternoon shift. It had started badly with a number of domestic incidents early on, mainly drink related, followed by various occurrences of anti-social behaviour, mainly involving teenagers. Then they had got held up for hours on a job where they had a prospective *jumper*. The male in question had been threatening to throw himself off the roof of a high-rise building and had had to be talked down by trained negotiators. The two partners had been limited in their duties to crowd control below.

Kristen said goodnight after changing out of her uniform in the locker room and headed home. Lauren though idled and took her time changing into her *civvies,* as the station was quiet at this time as most of the night shift were already out on jobs that had been called in earlier. She wondered into the main office and saw that Lucas and Chohan must have gone home too as their desks were vacant. Idly, she sidled up to their corner and

casually looked at the files they had left on top of their work tables.
Checking around her constantly, to avoid being seen, she carefully removed certain documents of interest and strolled over to the photocopier. After making numerous copies, she returned them to the files on their desks and headed out. The few officers milling about the station had been busy and hadn't seen a thing. Lauren felt slightly guilty about doing this, but she wanted to be a detective one day and after all, *curiosity was the mother of invention! Her research was crying out for more information, like a desire that needed to be satiated.*
After an uneventful drive home, she laid the photocopied documents on the coffee table, along with the notes from her previous research and went to the kitchen to pour herself a glass of wine. Returning, she tied her long blond hair back in a ponytail to prevent herself fiddling with it as she worked, which was a nervous habit of hers. Sipping her drink she perused the various papers and tried to make more connections to add to the work that she had done previously regarding the victims of electro-shock therapy at Willowbrook:-

1. Harold Webb – a prolific paedophile and rapist – Jess' first trip described him trying to attack her.
2. Arthur Cooper – a member of the Order of Val Kyrie (weird cult) who was implicated in the murders of the Chesterfield family – In John's first trip he visits an old stately home and sees the corpses of Reginald and Jemima Chesterfield and their two daughters Elizabeth and Mary and their only son Jack.
3. Elizabeth Shaw
4. John Carey
5. Max Clifford
- John and Sarah described their trip together and how they were involved in a 50s robbery- all three

above went on to more serious crimes and eventually ended up in Willowbrook after pleading insanity.
6. Stephen Parkins- an ex-RAF fighter pilot during WWII – suffered 80% first degree burns when he was shot down and ended up in Willowbrook due to his deteriorating mental condition- link with Rick Clay's death
7. Alan Parker- murdered his wife and lover by bludgeoning them to death with a baseball bat and claimed insanity and ended up in Willowbrook – link with detective Noble's death
8. Andrew Murray- leader of the Order of Val Kyrie – witnessed murdering a young female by Jess and Sarah on their trip- they describe the murder weapon as a dagger with an ornate carved handle consisting off three embossed intertwining snakes set with emeralds- also he wore a ring with this same emblem.
9. William Cox
10. Rupert Williams
- Both the above spent over ten years together living in Africa and suffered nervous breakdowns after losing numerous members of their party whilst on safari – link to John Anderson's and inspector Briggs' deaths
11. Alan Pratt – no information

Only the last person was unaccounted for- Alan Pratt. During her dinner-break that night, she and Lauren had returned to the station about 8pm and she had spent half an hour checking various computer files for any information she could find out about him. All that she had managed to discover was that he had worked as a junior accountant at a prestigious firm and for reasons unknown had jumped in front of a subway train one fateful day, clearly attempting suicide.
However, for some reason he had mistimed his jump and had hit the side of the train causing him

multiple injuries, none of which were life threatening- mainly severe bruising and broken ribs. Shortly afterwards, he had been omitted to Willowbrook due to his obvious mental health difficulties; he had protested against this and calmly argued his case but lost as the authorities are not prone to side with anyone who attempts to take their own life.

As she studied the various papers and documents with concentrated determination, her pretty features were sullied somewhat by her down-turned expression. Then she found a connection whilst looking at the post-mortem results of Sam. A particular sentence rang a bell in her head immediately: *the deceased has been decapitated and dismembered which is consistent with those injuries suffered in road accidents or train suicides.* There it was a plausible link between Alan Pratt and Sam Matheson. Why Sam had died and Alan had not she couldn't fathom but the connection was there nonetheless.

Next, she looked at the results for Chris Turner and again a particular phrase was of interest: *his pulverised remains are inconclusive as to the cause of death but consistent with being run-over by a truck or other heavy moving object.* So, in other words most likely a road accident. Now she knew that John Anderson had ridden a high-end motorbike and also, from her first-hand experience, had witnessed the results of fatal collisions involving such bikes with large vehicles many times before. The link was there, however tentative.

The best was yet to come in regard to Megan Cliff's death and her friend, now in custody, Beth Maloney who had appeared on the chair with her dead friend clutching an ornate dagger. The weapon's blade was covered in blood. Three intertwining snakes were embossed on the handle which was set with emeralds in alabaster. The lab results read: two

types of blood had been found- one a positive match for Megan and the other had been identified as a former resident of Willowbrook, an Andrew Murray who had died there whilst being administered electro-shock therapy. He was a known member of some weird religious cult called the *Order of Val Kyrie.*
Not only that, thought Lauren but it appeared from Chohan's notes that Beth claimed to have witnessed Murray executing her friend by slitting her throat with the same said dagger and then later raping her in his private quarters. *The swabs a doctor had taken from her vagina and the robe she had been wearing had come back a positive match to the DNA of Murray! It doesn't get much better than this*; Lauren thought smiling and taking a large gulp of wine to celebrate.
She added the extra information that she had obtained to the end of her list:-

11. Alan Pratt – accountant who attempted suicide by trying to jump in front of a train
12. Above - link to death of Sam Matheson
13. Chris Turner – possible link with John Anderson- may have died during a motorbike accident
14. Megan Cliff – throat slit by Andrew Murray- witnessed by her friend Beth Maloney -his DNA matches that found on the robe that Beth was wearing and the swabs taken from her vagina
15. Lee Chiles – nailed to a wall with metallic shard from a rusted bed-frame- in inverted crucifix position- cause unknown
16. Charlie Baker – eyes gouged out causing severe trauma- perpetrator unknown

Lauren smiled enlightening her features whilst she sipped her wine and regarded her handiwork- *I'm really getting somewhere,* she thought. She tidied up her notes and the various documents and papers on the coffee table. Finishing her wine, she replaced the now empty glass by the kitchen sink and headed off to bed.

Detective Lucas awoke the next morning, alone as he was divorced, with a splitting headache and a dry mouth due to dehydration. He rubbed the sleep from his eyes to find that he was still fully clothed, lying back on his couch with a half-empty bottle of scotch and numerous empty bottles of beer on the low table to the side of him. He groaned and grimaced with the pain of his hangover- it hurt his head even to move. Closing his eyes once more, he thought about calling in sick but the call would have to wait as he immediately passed out again.

Later that morning, he was awoken by his doorbell ringing incessantly. He groaned and tried to get up and, with difficulty, stumbled towards the door of his apartment and opened it. Chohan's rebuking frown greeted him and he staggered back towards the couch whilst his partner consoled him with, "Hey man, don't worry I've been covering for you. Heavy night, I take it?"

Lying back down Lucas groaned, "It's this case man."

"Tell me about it", replied Chohan, "Look, I've brought coffee and doughnuts when you're ready for them... I'll check by on you later, okay partner?" he finished heading off and quietly closing the door behind him whilst Lucas went back to sleep.

Chohan drove back to the station as he wanted to do some research himself on Willowbrook and its former residents. Seeing his partner in such a state was no big surprise as they had worked together for years now and it was a fairly regular occurrence. *Lucas had never quite got over his wife leaving him, that was for sure.*

Later that day, Lucas finally turned up for work looking rough and dishevelled but no-one noticed as

that was not unusual either. He went over to his corner desk and joined Chohan who was busy looking over the old Anderson case files. It seemed that particular case was as baffling as the one they were currently working on.
"You know most of the victims in the Anderson case claimed to have sat on the chair and been transported to another dimension in time which is similar to Beth Maloney's account", Chohan mused.
"Don't tell me you're starting to believe that rubbish, are you? They're all just delusional *fruitcakes*- that's all there is to it, nothing more sinister than that", Lucas replied grumpily.
"Well, I think one of us should try sitting on it, just to discount the theory anyway, however absurd", Chohan suggested.
"You can count me out", answered Lucas, "I'm not sitting on that blood and gore stained decrepit looking chair", his partner stated decisively.
"What do you mean? I thought you had it cleaned... Don't you remember yesterday's interview- it was spotless", Chohan replied confused.
"Why would I do that? No, I didn't notice either", Lucas answered wearily.
"C'mon let's take a look", his partner said getting up and he reluctantly followed him into the interview room. Inside, he could clearly see that Chohan was right- it was spotless. *Weird that he hadn't noticed it before,* he thought. "You see!" Chohan stated happily, "Okay, who's going to give it a try?"
"Be my guest, partner", replied Lucas dolefully sipping his coffee.
Chohan grinned and pretended to be greatly excited by the prospect, making a show of himself before he finally sat down. Lucas dropped his coffee cup in shock as his partner disappeared almost instantaneously before his very eyes. Whilst his half-empty cup hit the floor, spilling out its lukewarm contents all over the carpet.

Chohan awoke from what appeared to a rushing swirling dream to find that he was leaning back on a safety-rope halfway up a sheer mountain rock-face. He immediately panicked as he glimpsed the large vertical drop beneath him, nearly losing his foot and handholds that held him to the rock. Luckily, he just managed to maintain his grip. Pressing his head close to the rock-face he started shaking uncontrollably and felt unable to move for quite a while. *Where the hell was he? More importantly, how on earth had he managed to get where he was? Rock climbing was the last thing on earth he wanted to be doing with his confirmed case of vertigo.*

To his horror, he suddenly leant back from the sheer face and shifted his weight slightly as one of his feet moved up to a higher position and tested it. Within moments, he began rising upwards; his hands also automatically it seemed seeking out higher holds further up. After repeating the process several times on the trot he found that he had risen a further ten feet or so. Then he took out a safety clip and wedged it into a gap in the rock and attached his rope to it as he did so. It quickly dawned on him that *he was not the one doing the climbing, it was someone else. At least they seem to know what they were doing!*

Thanking God but also wishing he could close his eyes at the same time- he was unable to do so as he was, in fact, seeing with someone else's vision. Further up they climbed, higher and higher making Chohan feel sick with fear and worry. He knew if they fell from such a great height they wouldn't stand a chance. The safety rope, at least, made him feel some reassurance. The sun beat down strongly above them and it felt unbearably hot and stifling with very little in the way of a breeze to cool them. The person clearly felt it too as he unnervingly kept letting go of a handhold to wipe sweat from his brow onto his shirt sleeve.

The climb seemed never-ending as they proceeded to go higher and higher, step-by-step. What felt like hours later, the man looked up and Chohan could see that they were perhaps only thirty feet or so from the summit. *Thank God,* thought Chohan, cheered somewhat by the end now being in sight. Unfortunately, just then one of the climber's feet slipped and he lost his handholds too simultaneously. Time seemed to stand still as they fell in slow motion with Chohan screaming every millisecond inside the person's head. Then a stomach churning jolt as the safety rope held on the grip below.

Luckily, the detective was unable to pee; otherwise they probably would have been soaking wet by now. Looking up again, it appeared they had fallen only about ten feet but it had seemed like an eternity in freefall. The climber shrugged and readjusted his equipment before proceeding on with the ascent. Chohan promised himself that he would never climb anything except for stairs ever again. The man climbed higher and higher and after what felt like an immeasurable length of time, they had past their previous height and gone further up the mountain. *Never again,* the detective thought, *never again.*

Steadily, they continued this time the man seemed to be taking no chances and securing extra grips in between the gaps in the rock; *he clearly hadn't enjoyed their fall either.* On and on they went, sweating profusely in what appeared to be the mid-afternoon sun. Finally, they reached the last few feet of the climb and Chohan cheered inside the man's mind as they reached the summit. They dragged themselves up onto the fairly uneven but flat top surface and rolled onto their back, taking deep breaths as they did so, panting for much needed air.

After a short while, the climber got to his feet and stood and looked out at what, Chohan had to admit was an incredible view. They could see miles into the distance, over what appeared to be a whole range of rocky and irregular mountains; blue skies and fluffy white clouds all around them. The detective felt the man's pride and ecstasy at his achievement and gloried himself in it too. Finally, the climber shrugged and took a second rope off his shoulders, one end which he wound round a large rock on the summit and the other which he attached to his harness via clips. It looked like they were about to abseil down which, at least Chohan thought should be a lot quicker, even though uncomfortably scary at the same time.

6.

Lucas stood mesmerised looking incomprehensively in utter shock and confusion at the chair in front of him. *How was it possible? Chohan had been there one minute and then suddenly he was gone the next. What the hell's going on? Am I losing my mind finally?* These thoughts were whizzing and spinning around his mind, seemingly unable to break loose and free him from this nightmare. He found that he couldn't even move or speak; all he could do was just stand there in bewilderment.

Lauren and Kristen turned up at the police department just at that time, for their late afternoon shift. Kristen happened to glance through the interview room one-way window to see Lucas just standing there in front of the chair and as still as a statue. Below him was a plastic coffee cup on its side and a large splattering of a coffee stain all around it on the grey carpet. "Hey, check out Lucas!" she ejaculated.

Lauren came over and peered through the glass to see what her colleague meant. "What the hell's wrong with him? He's not even moving!" she exclaimed bemused.

"You tell me partner... I always knew he was a nutcase!" Kristen replied shrugging.

"He's certainly a weirdo; I'll give you that... C'mon let's get to work", Lauren answered heading towards the door and their patrol car outside. Her partner nodded grinning at her and followed her out of the station.

Chohan grimaced inside the man's head as he braced himself over the sheer vertical drop which appeared to be some two hundred feet or more and leant backwards over the edge. His weight pulled the harness tort around his midriff as he braced himself to begin the descent. Pausing slightly to make a few adjustments to his equipment, he then leapt backwards suddenly, straight out into the air away from the rock-face. The detective cried out in silent fear in his mind as the climber released the rope in short distances and they hopped down the sheer slope.

Gaining confidence, the man took larger leaps into the air and descended greater distances; instead of ten, he dropped fifteen or perhaps even twenty feet at one time, his feet bouncing off the rock-face as he did so. The detective hated every minute of what he was witnessing as every leap sent his stomach racing into his mouth and he felt like throwing up in abject fear and loathing of his current predicament. Unfortunately for Chohan, they still had at least over a hundred and fifty feet left to reach the ground.

They took another leap and then another but this time something went wrong and the safety rope above came loose after a sudden jolt and Chohan despairingly found that they were in freefall once more, and rapidly accelerating towards the ground below. This time the climber too lost his cool and uttered a piercing shriek of fear and desperation into the air around then as they fell. The detective was already screaming though, hysterically and unabatedly as he too recognised the now inevitable outcome.

They seemed to fall forever and even twisted around a few times as they did so. Chohan sensed the man had lost consciousness but unfortunately, he had not and he was still hopelessly aware of what was going on. The detective even found a short period of peace and tranquillity as they rushed downwards; the rock-face now a blur with the air around gently buffeting them and caressing them as they fell. The impact as they hit the ground was a minute fraction of excruciating pain until Chohan felt nothing whatsoever, except strangely he found himself rising upwards into the ether.

Lucas had finally managed to free himself from his trance and had moved but not very far; only to the nearby desk and taken a seat beside it overlooking the now dreaded chair. He had lost all concept of time and just sat there where he was with barely a thought passing through his mind and it seemed as though he had hit a roadblock in consciousness, beyond which he was unable to pass. *Why did he have to get assigned to this damn case?* It was literally making him question his own sanity.

Then he thought about Beth Maloney. *It appeared that she had in fact been raped, the problem being the perpetrator Murray had been dead for more than twenty years! Contemplating the implications of that alone was enough to drive anyone crazy.* Not only that, but now no-one was allowed to see her except specially trained police counsellors. Apparently, she had broken down yet again when they had finally began to believe, at least some, of her version of events.

The shit had hit the fan big time and Lucas felt covered in it. *Now his partner was missing as well just by virtue of sitting on that damn chair!* He was at a dead-end, with no way past; no detours just stuck firmly where he was. *How could he even mention this to anyone, let alone his superiors?* If he did, he expected that they'd cart him off to the nearest nuthouse, lock him up and throw away the key. The worst of it being that, in their shoes, he would do the same.

Where do I go from here? The truth was, he didn't have a clue, so he just sat there where he was doing nothing. Eventually, a female officer came in to check that he was okay as he didn't look well at all.

He just made some lame excuse as to the reason why and assured her with a weak attempt at a smile that nothing was wrong and she left. How long he sat there he really didn't know, or care for that matter.

Suddenly, he noticed some shape materialising before him on the chair and, after a few seconds, he could clearly make out it was Chohan. Lucas breathed a deep sigh of relief and was about to get up and greet his partner as he reappeared momentarily, as he was before. Unfortunately though, his body shape changed dramatically a second later into a malformed crushed and broken wreck. Chohan's head had caved in and parts of his skull and brain were clearly visible. In fact, he was hardly recognisable at all, covered in his own blood and gore but the suit he had been wearing was.

This was all too much for Lucas and he vomited on the table in front of him; the sick spraying and deflecting off the table-top onto his own jacket, chair and shoes. His partner's pulverised body fell face down onto the floor with a horrible crunching squelching sound which made him throw-up even more. Luckily, he had not eaten much that day and so there was not that much left to come back up, so soon he found himself retching violently and producing that horrible green stomach lining fluid which tastes just as bad as it looks.

Lauren and Kristen had just arrived at their next job of that evening, an all too common drunken domestic incident. Getting out of the patrol car they rushed to the front door and banged on it; there was clearly a great deal of commotion going on inside. The shouting and screaming was clearly loud enough to be audible at the far end of the street, Lauren surmised as she rapped on the door once more.

"Open up! Police!" she shouted.
She repeated this call several times before a woman finally answered the door with very slurred speech and was clearly so drunk, she could hardly stand up. A moment later, the female collapsed on the floor in front of them and Lauren and Kristen had to step over her body to proceed inside. Going into the main living room, they found utter mayhem ensuing. Two other females were fighting viciously in a corner, clawing and scratching at one another whilst trying to tear out each other's hair. On the other side of the room two males were drunkenly fighting but their punches were weak and not really connecting with each other.
Quickly prioritising, Kristen lunged forward to break the two females apart whilst Lauren headed over to the males to calm them down. After a lot more screaming and shouting the two officers finally managed to placate the situation and one of the females was cuffed and arrested for assaulting Kristen whilst she intervened. The males luckily were too drunk to be much of a problem and very soon, they both passed out on the couch on top of one another. The other female was directed to sit on a side chair in the kitchen, where she immediately starting crying.
Kristen radioed for an ambulance as clearly most of them needed checking over even though it might turn out that they just needed to sleep it off. Meanwhile Lauren had locked the detainee in the back of the police car. Eventually, some paramedics arrived and decided to take the female who had fallen over at the door to the hospital just in case as she might have banged her head. The others were pronounced okay to be left alone to sleep it off, so Lauren and Kristen headed back to the station with one drunken female.
Arriving at the police department, they booked her in and then dragged her as she was still being

aggressive, abusive and uncooperative to the cells and locked her up. All the way, the female swore at them but they had heard it all so many times before, it was now like water off a duck's back to them.

"What a bitch!" said Kristen as they left the cells and headed towards the main offices down various corridors.

Lauren nodded, "Looks like it's going to be *one of those nights...*" she sighed.

"Yeah, same old shit different day", replied Kristen as they walked out into the main block where the interview rooms were to find a lot of officers gathered around the first one, where the chair was.

"What's going on?" she asked one of the male officers who was nearby.

"Detective Lucas has been arrested and taken for psychiatric evaluation... he was found covered in his own vomit next to the dead body of detective Chohan who looked like he'd fallen off the top of a high rise building or something... Whatever you do, don't look through the viewing window- there's shit everywhere!" he ejaculated.

Lauren and Kristen tried to find out more but no-one seemed to know much else and the room itself had now been sealed off, for the use of detectives only. However, the two female partners couldn't resist a quick look through the one-way glass and they grimaced at the scene that confronted them: blood, gore, body-fluids and sick everywhere. Lauren noticed that the chair itself strangely seemed to be untainted now.

They headed back towards their desks to fill in their report of the previous incident. "Did you notice the chair- it should've been covered with all kinds of shit but it looked like it had been it a different room- not a mark or stain on it... How's that possible?" Lauren asked bemused.

"Beats me partner... You would've expected some of blood stains at least especially bearing in mind the previous incident with Beth Maloney... Now I come to think about it, it doesn't seem right... I mean when I saw it the other day it was covered in blood and gore- so who the hell has cleaned it and destroyed vital evidence? It just doesn't make any sense", Kristen replied equally confused.
"Tell me about it", replied her partner as they sat at their respective desks.

The demon creature stood alone in cell three of the basement at Willowbrook contemplating his situation. Thanks to that *stupid witch*, Jess Anderson, he had managed to come through the portal to this world through her spells and incantations. *Little did most fools on earth know but black magic actually works and there is no such thing as white magic! Well, at least that bitch and her dumb husband John were now paying a very serious price for what they had done in the vilest corners of hell.* He knew if he was there now, their *screams and torture would be obscene and extremely entertaining to all who were there.*
The problem was that only he had managed to get through the vortex she had created, as there had been insufficient time for others to follow. He needed the chair back so he could use his powers on it to re-open the portal but, of course, this would require more blood sacrifice. However, that he didn't mind one bit as to him, such things were pleasurable. The other main difficulty was that he couldn't just go wandering about town due to the way he looked: reptilian with armoured dark skin, jagged teeth, large claws and the horrific looking face of a monstrous devil with searing red eyes that seemed aflame when he spoke.

Yes, clearly such an appearance would no go down well with most humans except for the odd few devil worshippers and Satanists. He presumed correctly that the police had taken the chair to the nearest main department in the vicinity. *It was just a question of how he was going to get it back...* He pondered the various possibilities open to him with a vile sneer on his hideously corrupt and malevolent face. *Little did anyone know but he was actually a King of hell; one of their vilest leaders with eighty legions of demons under his command.* He laughed aloud at the *ignorance of the human fools!*

Lauren and Kristen filed their report and headed back out onto the streets for yet another job; this time it was an emergency call: a mass drunken brawl was taking place in the city centre. All available units had been called due to the severity of the incident. Kristen flicked on the siren, then the flashing blue lights and they accelerated off at high speed towards the violence. On the way, Lauren cursed at some slow moving drivers who seemed blissfully unaware of their surroundings and neglected to get out of their way.

Reaching the scene, they quickly saw that it was carnage. A mass brawl was taking place in the streets and officers already there, were struggling to deal with the numbers. They quickly added themselves to their ranks, as well as another few patrol cars that turned up around the same time. Batons raised, they headed into the fight. Many drunken men had to be beaten to the ground before they'd submit but eventually calm ensued. Many arrests were made and the culprits taken from the scene to custody in a large van.

The aftermath was a scene of utter devastation and wreckage: some cars had been set alight and had subsequently blown up as their fuel tanks had exploded. Shop windows had been smashed and there was blood everywhere. Many ambulances were needed to deal with all the casualties; ironically a lot of the injuries being caused by the police themselves. Finally, everyone was placated and Lauren and Kristen left to go to another less urgent job.

The King had considered his options but only one of them stood out: he needed to possess a human and take their form so that he could access the police station. All he needed now was the right victim; anyone prone to delving into the black arts or any such form of worship would be ideal. He could sense nothing for a while, in the immediate vicinity anyway. Then suddenly, his dark prayers were answered: there was some kind of gathering not too far away where a group of youths were beginning to perform a séance. *That's exactly what I needed!* He thought as he made his way out of Willowbrook.

It was just after 11.30pm when Lauren and Kristen's next job came through. That was typical- they were due to clock off at 12pm and now, if they were unlucky, they might be tied up for hours at this new incident. The extra overtime pay was nice but sometimes, especially after a long shift, you just needed to get home. This time it was some kind of road accident involving at least two vehicles but not much more was known at the time the call came through.

To be on the safe side, in case of injury, they treated it as an emergency and headed at speed towards the scene. When they arrived, they almost wished they hadn't as it was a head on collision between two vehicles that were almost unrecognisable due to the severity of the impact. It turned out that the

sole occupant of one vehicle had not been wearing his seat belt and thus, had been catapulted through his windscreen with what appeared to be vociferous force. His lifeless blood-splattered crushed body ending up in the road, some distance ahead.
The occupants of the other vehicle were wearing their seatbelts but the steering column had crushed into the driver on impact and the airbag seemed to have smothered the passenger. So that was three dead on arrival. They both groaned as they surveyed the wreckage and lifeless bodies; they were more than likely to be at the scene for hours until the night-shift relief crews turned up at the scene to relieve them.

It was a quarter past midnight when the demon turned up outside the house having skulked the mile or so distance through the shadows. He peered through various windows cautiously, not wanting to be seen, until he found a view of them in the living room. They were gathered about a low table, with all the letters of the alphabet drawn on single pieces of paper in a circle, inside of which was a glass and two further single pieces of paper which held the words: *yes* or *no.*
In the room, he could see a group of four teenagers, possibly about eighteen or nineteen years old. It appeared to be two couples as there were two boys and two girls. The King's hearing was way beyond any mortal and he could easily understand with clarity any word they said even though he was currently outside. He focused and listened intently on the proceedings with a mixture of amusement and expectation.

"Do we have to do this?" groaned one of the females; a pretty girl with short blond hair wearing tight shorts and a thin blouse.

"Stop being a pussy Pris... You're so lame- you never want to do anything!" The partner of the other girl replied.
"Jack, are you going to let him speak to me like that?" she retorted at her boyfriend, a blond curly haired hippy-type in a loose shirt and jeans.
"Hey calm down Pris", he replied, "Carl's just joking around that's all, aren't you Carl?" he finished giving his friend the evil eye.
His friend shrugged, "Yeah I'm just messing Pris, just messing."
"Are we going to get this party started?" interjected a slim pretty brunette with long hair as she dished out some bourbon into a number of shot glasses placed in front of her.
"Now that's just one of the reasons I love you so much Patty!" Carl ejaculated reaching for one of the glasses.
They all downed a number of drinks before finally it seemed they were ready, with even Pris having calmed down somewhat due to the effects of the alcohol. They also had numerous bottles of beer on the go at the same time, with even more empty bottles lying on their sides around the room and under the table.
"Okay, here we go! Quiet please everyone!" announced Jack as he turned an empty glass over and placed it in the middle of the table. "Is there anybody there?" he began ushering them all to put their forefingers on top of the glass. Nothing happened so he repeated the phrase, as it happened, three times before the glass began to move. It slid across the table surface from the direct centre towards the word *yes* and then back again where it again rested.
"Holy shit!" shouted Carl impressed, "It actually works!"
"Didn't I tell you buddy?" Jack replied knowingly.

"One of you is just moving the glass!" interjected Pris, clearly unhappy about the proceedings.
"No we're not! Stop being such a prude Pris, I told you many a time that it works", Patty groaned chastising her friend.
Pris felt the unsubtle vehemence behind her words and thus remained silent as Jack continued questioning the spirit, whoever he or she might be.
"Are you evil?" he asked.

Outside, the King smirked to himself as he made the glass move over to *no.* He was feeling immeasurably pleased with himself as he realised that tonight he would, most likely, get the body or *vessel* that he wanted but clearly, it looked like he was going to have a lot of fun along the way. *Nothing wrong with enjoying yourself whilst conducting business, is there?* He thought leering lasciviously at the group and pondering which one of them he wanted most.

"There you see Pris, it's not evil, so you've got nothing to worry about", Carl added as the glass moved back to the centre of the table. She replied by giving him a dirty look to which he just laughed.
Jack ignoring them continued, "Do you have a message for anyone here?"
This time the glass seemed to move even more rapidly under their joined fingertips towards *yes* and then back to the middle of the table where it again, stood still. Most of them by this time were beginning to feel frightened although none of them wished to admit it. Some of them could feel the hairs on the back of their necks starting to rise up and tingle.
"Who is the message for?" Jack carried on.
Again, the glass moved quickly over the polished wooden surface and began to spell out letters which Jack called out one-by-one as it did so. "P", he

began the continued with, "R", next it was "I", and lastly, "S", before the glass returned to the centre and stopped.
"Shit! That means you Pris!" Carl exclaimed happily.
"You're just moving the glass, all of you! Just to wind me up!" she retorted unamused.
"Sugar, honestly we're not", replied Jack to his girlfriend almost condescendingly.
"Yeah, I'm not moving it", interjected Patty, "My finger's hardly touching it... it's clearly moving by itself."
"Me neither", added Carl, "Hey, did you notice how fast it was moving? It's never moved that quickly when I've done them before!" he finished.
"Okay quiet guys", interrupted Jack as he proceeded, "What is your message for Pris?"
Again, they didn't need to wait long before the glass started moving rapidly from letter-to-letter. This time Carl chose to voice the letters aloud as the glass moved to them one-by-one, always returning to the centre of the table in between choices.
"S", he began followed by, "U", then "C", then, "K" and then waited as the glass seemed to have paused momentarily. "M", he continued then, "Y" and again he found the glass had stopped. Shortly afterwards, it continued and Carl carried on, "C", then, "O", then, "C" and finally, "K". He laughed hysterically as he realised the message was, *Suck my cock.*
Patty found this highly amusing too whilst Jack had to fight off the tears of laughter which were streaming down his face.
"You see! You're just making fun of me! How could you Jack? You're meant to be my boyfriend!" she stormed heading out of the room, clearly upset.

The demon was currently trying to contain his mirth after pulling that stunt. Tears of laughter streamed down his reptilian features as he struggled desperately not to make a sound. When he had finally managed to calm down, he realised he had made his choice: *it had to be Pris. What a prize specimen she was! He couldn't wait to get inside her, literally!* This thought sent him into hysterics again and he quickly backed away from the window in case they heard something.

Inside, Jack was currently rebuking Carl, "Why did you have to do that?" he said annoyed with his best friend.

"What do you mean? It wasn't me! I thought it must be you!" responded Carl laughing.

Jack sighed as he regarded his friend. "Sometimes, you know, you can be a right idiot!" he stormed at him as he left the room to find Pris.

"Hey it wasn't me!" Carl called after him but he had gone.

"You really didn't?" Patty whispered towards him.

"Scout's honour, hope to die and all that rubbish... No really it wasn't!" he finished in a more serious tone.

Patty stared at him fully in his eyes for a few moments before accepting he was telling the truth. "Well if you didn't and neither did Jack, who did?" she wondered.

"Guess it was a dark spirit or something", Carl mused.

"Yeah, I guess", replied Patty dubiously.

In the kitchen at the back of the house, Jack was trying to console Pris. He had assured her it wasn't him and he agreed with her that it was most likely Carl just messing about. "You know what he's like", he stated matter-of-factly.

"Yeah I do", she replied, "It's exactly the kind of thing he would do!"

"Look he's promised me he won't do it again, can't you come back and give it one more try? Please, for me", Jack said whilst holding her in his arms and gently kissing her bare neck from behind.
She turned to face him and they embraced kissing each other lovingly for a while and finally she acquiesced and went back with him to the living room. As they returned to the room, Jack gave Carl a penetrating stare warning him non-verbally not to say anything more. His friend took the hint and said nothing whilst Patty just welcomed them back amicably and they resumed the séance.

Outside, the demon returned to the window and grinned when he saw that they had changed seating positions and Pris now had her back to him which was just the way he wanted it. If he was to possess her he needed her to do the séance alone as the four of them together offered each other at least some protection if not much. Carl and Patty were currently facing him and Jack was seated side-on to the window where he was.
"What do you want?" he clearly heard Jack ask.
This time he made sure that the glass didn't move whilst he used his dark powers to command Carl and Patty to look at the window. *Look now*, he spoke in his mind. On cue, they both looked towards him and he gave them a powerful hypnotic stare, which took a lot of his energy to do so, but it achieved the required result as they were both immediately put into a trance. *Two down, one to go*, he thought.
Now he had to hurry before Pris noticed anything was wrong. He made the glass start moving but very slowly this time and fortunately both Jack and his target were calling out the letters together. He heard them both say, *Y*, then, *O*, before he stalled the glass. *Look at me* he commanded Jack who casually turned towards him and was too instantaneously

put into a trance. *His prey was now his for the taking.* He let the glass move once more and heard Pris on her own say, *U*, the first word is *YOU!*
Her eyes changed colour from their normal blue to red momentarily and then back again. She got up from the table and walked into the kitchen where she opened a draw near to the sink. She removed a large serrated edged knife and went back to the living room. There she casually slit the throats of all of her friends whilst they were still under the trance. The three saw and felt nothing and fell to the floor, one after the other, as she dealt out the lethal blows and the living room floor became quickly covered with blood.
Smiling now, Pris wiped the blood of the knife onto the couch before placing it in her handbag and exiting the house. Leaving the lifeless bodies behind her, she suddenly remembered something and casually walked back inside. In the living room once more, she delved into Jack's pockets and took out what she had been searching for –his car keys. Then she left the house and got into his Ford Mustang. She turned the key in the ignition whilst simultaneously revving the engine which roared back at her. Pris accelerated hard and drove at high speed towards the police department.

7.

It was just after 1am and there were very few officers manning the police station as most of the night shift were out on jobs. All that remained was a few crews who were filing reports after detaining suspects in custody and the odd desk sergeant or inspector. One male officer was just leaving the station on his own when a pretty girl with short blond hair wearing a thin blouse and shorts approached him.
"Officer I need your help", she said earnestly.
"What's the problem sweetheart?" he asked trying his luck.
"You are!" Pris declared as she withdrew the knife from her bag and rammed it straight into his chest, twisting it as she did so.
A look of shock and horror was clearly visible on his face and he groaned as blood poured out of his mouth and he dropped to the ground dead. Wasting no time, Pris removed his revolver from its holster and headed up the stairs to the police department's main double-doors and went inside. A single officer was manning the reception desk; he looked up as she approached and was just about to ask if he could help her when she shot him twice in the chest and he slid from his chair dead.
Pris quickly turned a corner and headed down a corridor. Two officers that had been alerted by the gunshots came running towards her. As they were about to draw their weapons she shot them both. The female one was struck in the head and died instantly whilst her male colleague was hit in the groin. He fell to the floor grimacing and crying out in agony as she walked casually over to him and shot him in the head from point-blank range. Blood,

bits of skull and brain splattered on the floor around him.

Pausing Pris took his gun as well and continued down the corridor brandishing two weapons out in front of her. A female sergeant fired off a round in her direction, but due to her anxiety, she missed and Pris blasted her with both revolvers and then stepped over her lifeless body. She shot further senior officers in their offices as she went past their open doorways. Hearing the echo of numerous footsteps running towards her, she ducked into one of the offices as three policeman carrying assault rifles suddenly rushed past.

Casually stepping out into the corridor, she shot all three numerous times in the back using both revolvers once more. Throwing them away, she picked up an assault rifle and headed towards the main office complex in more of a crouched position. Pris took great care to peep round every corner she came to in case there were others. Continuing she reached the main open plan office area to find some more senior officers still at their desks. *Why they hadn't reacted was beyond her.* Raising her weapon she sprayed them both with lead and they both crashed to the floor.

Entering the area, she noticed the interview rooms further ahead off a side-corridor and headed that way turning to shoot another officer that had appeared nearby. A few suspects had been handcuffed to some benches outside them and they pleaded with her to release them. Pris paused and shot them mercilessly in cold blood. They all fell to the floor with their arms still held by the constraints and their blood everywhere.

Aware that she did not have much time before more police officers arrived, she quickly looked through the viewing windows of the rooms just in case the chair was there otherwise she would have to check every damn room in the place until she found it.

Luckily, there it was in room one. She went inside and grabbed it dragging it along the floor behind her with the assault rifle now held awkwardly by her other arm. Pris retraced her steps laboriously this time as the chair was heavy and cumbersome to move. However, as she was now possessed by the demon her strength had become much greater than before. Thus, it didn't take her very long to reach the main entrance. Pris was just about to wrestle the chair through the doors when she heard sirens and rapidly approaching patrol cars.

Leaving the chair where it was, she went outside and took up a crouched position at the top of the stairs using a side wall as some cover. She waited until three police cars had arrived almost simultaneously and six officers in total ran towards the building. Pris casually aimed down her sight and shot them all, spraying them with bullets over and over until the weapon trigger just clicked and fired no more. Discarding the rifle, she went back inside and grabbed the chair and carried it down the stairs.

Laying it down on the ground, she checked the police cars to find one with the keys still in the ignition otherwise she would have had to take them from one of the bodies. Taking the keys she opened the boot and then returned to fetch the chair. Minutes later, she threw it in the trunk and leaving it open she got inside and drove off at high speed totally unable to see out of the back. Without thinking further, she headed towards Willowbrook.

It was just before 2am and Lauren and Kristen were still at the scene of the road traffic accident (RTA) directing traffic around the smashed up vehicles which had been pushed to one side. Earlier, the bodies had been removed and a lot of debris swept up to clear the road. Suddenly, the emergency call came through that the police department had been attacked, code red- all units. Rushing back to their patrol car, they got in and Kristen quickly turned on the siren whilst Lauren drove at speed towards their headquarters.

Shortly afterwards, they arrived at the station to find a scene of utter devastation and complete pandemonium. It appeared an assault had taken place and numerous officers had been killed, all DOA. Some of their colleagues were crying, others were frantically rushing about and the rest were just slumped in chairs with their heads in their hands in total disbelief of the carnage they had discovered there.

Lauren and Kristen helped out and assisted as best they could with whatever tasks they were needed to perform. Both were struggling though in a state of confusion and incomprehension, as thoughts spun around their heads as to how and why such a massacre could have happened. They had no clue or even the vaguest idea or reason why; it was totally incomprehensible. Working through the night, they did their duty and were finally relieved about 6am after very close to a fourteen hour shift. Tired and totally fatigued, both mentally and physically, they headed home.

Pris parked as near as she could to Willowbrook's main gates without being visible to the patrol car that may or not still be guarding the entrance. Using one of the policemen's keys, she unlocked a gun compartment behind the handbrake and removed a shotgun and checked that it was loaded. After doing so she took off her clothes and walked naked towards the gates using both hands to hold the shotgun behind her in the small of her back.

Within a few minutes, she could see two male officers on patrol casually talking with one another,

their backs turned away from her. She approached until she was in earshot and then cried out desperately, “Help me please! I’ve been attacked!”
The officers turned and rushed towards her and Pris couldn’t help notice both of them looking at first her breasts and then her pussy in turn before directing their attention towards her face. One was just about to speak to offer assistance when she quickly revealed the shotgun and blasted them both in succession numerous times. Both of their bodies flew backwards due to the impact at close range and lay at the side of the road, dead.
She checked both of their pockets and found a set of keys and then got in their car and manoeuvred it away from the main gates which it had been blocking and turned off the engine. As Pris went back towards her vehicle, she absently decided to take one of the revolvers from one of their corpses. She got back in her car and drove at speed towards the main gates and succeeded in smashing though them.
However, the force of the impact had damaged her vehicle, which very nearly ground to a halt but fortunately just managed to hobble on as far as the main entrance of the old establishment, with smoke pouring out of the crumpled up bonnet. Getting out quickly, she removed the chair from the trunk and took it inside.

The next morning, a passing motorist reported two dead officers lying in the road outside the old Willowbrook mental institution and several units were despatched forthwith. Many officers though were still tied up at the police department where the press had caught wind of the story, via some leak, and turned up en masse. They were currently camped up impatiently outside awaiting the inevitable first statement from some high ranking official; they really didn't care who.

Outside Willowbrook's main entrance, officers Bukowski and Dick screeched to a halt and grimaced at the sight of their two dead colleagues. They arranged for an ambulance to remove the bodies and called in for back-up. Shortly afterwards, officers Orwell and Huxley arrived and joined them. After the bodies were taken from the scene, the four officers decided to proceed inside the gates and a few minutes later, located another missing patrol vehicle parked outside the building itself.

All four officers removed their weapons and portable flashlights and proceeded inside. Everyone at the department was by now well aware of the previous deaths that had occurred there and no-one was willing to take any chances. It was just after 8am that morning but the ground floor interior was still very gloomy due to the boarded up windows and it being a cloudy downcast day. However, their quick search of the floor yielded nothing so they all headed for the stairwell.

Bukowski and Dick opted to check the basement whilst directing Orwell and Huxley upstairs to investigate the higher levels. A dripping sound could be heard echoing around the stairwell emanating from somewhere below. Venturing down into what appeared to be a black pit with only their flashlights to guide them, the two officers proceeded with their descent. Reaching the bottom level they forced open the door which yielded unwillingly with a grating, screeching jarring sound which reverberated down the corridor in front of them.

They found the first two cells to be empty except for charred metal bed-frames, a broken toilet and sink. The stench down there was incredible; the worst smell you could ever imagine magnified again and again. They both grimaced and choked at the vile corruptness of the place and tried to breathe through their mouths only; this proved difficult as it was so abhorrent. They headed for the next cell, stumbling on various pieces of fallen masonry which seemed to line the corridor floor.

Looking inside the cell and entrance they could see various stains which were hard to make out in the dim light given off by their flashlights. In a far corner they saw the chair which had been placed against the wall. Bukowski tripped over the door which was lying in his path, having seemingly broken free of its hinges, and stumbled forward. Dick followed close behind him as they looked around; just the same rubbish as in the previous cells. They both aware of the case of the so-called ghost-hunters who had died in suspicious circumstances down there but all their equipment had been previously removed.

"Let's check the other rooms", said Dick.

"Hold on a sec, my leg's playing up again, let me just rest for a minute", replied Bukowski as he sat down on the chair.

Dick flicked his flashlight around the room, taking a second look around as his partner did so. Then he turned back towards him and stared dumbfoundedly at what was now an empty old chair. "What the fuck?" he said aloud.

Bukowski awoke from what had seemed like an unimaginable swirling, twisting dreamscape in which his body had been flying around at incredible speed, to find he was in what appeared to be some sort of mailroom. He could see that he was currently sorting mail laboriously into various pigeonholes in front of him. This seemed to go on for hours and yet he found that he couldn't get out of there. It dawned on him suddenly, that he was viewing the scene through someone else's vision as though he was sitting in their head looking out of their eye sockets.

Just then, a man came by and told him off for leaving his personal possessions in the space allocated for mailbags. "Do that again and expect your personal resignation letter on my desk by tomorrow morning", he threatened before walking off. The man whose body he seemed to be occupying gave, what was clearly his supervisor, the *finger* after he had left the room. Bukowski wished he could get out of there right this minute but disappointedly found that he was unable to do anything but watch.

Five minutes later, the man left the room and went into an office where he took a pen and a piece of paper from the table and wrote out a quick resignation letter which he signed and left where it was before leaving shortly afterwards. Then the man picked up a mailbag and headed out onto the streets, seemingly to deliver some mail. Within about twenty minutes of strenuous and laboured walking under the weight of the bag, Bukowski presumed they had reached the start of the round as the man began delivering mail.

After depositing letters at various houses along the street, he reached a point where he could see a man standing outside the front door of his house, further on up the street. Bukowski watched with interest as the postman who he appeared to be with, suddenly broke out into a sprint towards this particular man's mailbox situated at the end of his drive. Seeing this the man at the doorway followed suit and equally began to run.

What the hell's going on? Bukowski thought bemused. Soon he found out as his postman reached the mailbox just before the other man and deposited some *junk* mail inside of it before running off leaving the man swearing and gesticulating behind him in his wake. *Hilarious!* Bukowski thought laughing inside the man's head as they moved on. The postman was now sweating profusely both due to his previous exertions but also due to the midday sun and the pack on his shoulder and Bukowski felt every bit of his discomfort.

Finally, they seemed to be coming towards the end of the round, as the mailbag was clearly much lighter now, and the officer watched as the postman approached the next house where a dog seemed to be growling vociferously inside; having clearly smelt him from inside, on his approach to the doorway. Unfortunately, a woman opened the door just as he was about to post her mail and a German shepherd dog leapt into the air and snapped its jaws around his neck. Its bite pierced his jugular vein and blood spurted out everywhere.

Bukowski cried out in pain as the man's agony was relayed swiftly to his own cognisance. The police officer felt himself becoming weaker by the second, then stumbling about and falling over to the ground whilst the owner was desperately trying to call the dog off. However, it ignored her and carried on with its vicious attack making numerous further bites and horrifically goring the postman's body, Bukowski suddenly found that the pain had stopped and he was floating away up into the sky.

A large area had been taped off around the police department as it was all now, effectively a crime scene. Numerous members of the media were present outside the cordon, their vans all lined up alongside one another. Many news presenters were doing their first live bulletins, as the Chief of police had just given a brief press conference confirming only, that there had been a shootout and a number of officers had been killed; the gunman being still at large. Later, it would be revealed that eighteen officers had lost their lives in the line of duty in the early hours of that morning as well as two suspected criminals.

The news had caused a media frenzy and numerous reporters, photographers, cameramen, sound and lighting crews as well as presenters were rushing about, going to-and-fro on various assignments. As news stories went, this was about as *big* as it got and consequently all the national media were present. Such a massacre at a police station was almost unheard of and front-page news.

Dick couldn't believe what had happened. *Where the hell had his partner disappeared to?* Bukowski had sat down on that chair only moments ago and then he was nowhere to be seen. *He couldn't have left the cell, as I surely would've heard him go past,* he thought, as there was so much debris littered around the area. In a state of confusion and shock he just stood there motionless in front of the chair, his flashlight still focused on it.

"Don't move or make a sound", a female voice stated coldly from behind him. "If you do, I'll shoot you in the back", she continued. Dick did as she instructed and he heard her slowly step towards him; his hearing amplified by the lack of light. Soon he could sense that she was standing right behind him. He thought about turning to challenge her but swiftly decided against, as he was only a year away from retirement and not about to take any chances. Then he felt the barrel of a gun press into the small of his back.

"One wrong move and you're dead", she threatened.

Dick replied nervously, "Okay lady, take it easy."

"I told you not to speak- one more word and you're dead", she whispered in his ear as she took out the knife and pressed it against his throat. Pris ran the

blade slowly over his neck, only slightly piercing the skin as she did so. The policeman could feel his tears flow gently down his face. Dick was petrified and almost shaking with a mixture of adrenalin and fear, but at the same time, feeling impotent to do anything about it.
However, she seemed to lose interest in the knife and suddenly dropped it and its metallic blade clattered as it hit the stone floor and echoed all and reverberated all around the interior. Pris then shot him three times in the back and Dick dropped to the floor dead taking his unachieved retirement plans with him as he fell.

Upstairs Orwell and Huxley clearly heard the distinct sound of a gunshot as the small confines of the basement had served to amplify the sound. They were currently in the middle of checking the second floor, having found nothing on the first. Huxley automatically called for back-up via his radio. After which, they proceeded down the stairs to the basement moving slowly but surely with both their guns drawn.
The basement door grated and ground on the stone floor as they opened it; the sound despairingly loud so anyone who was down there would be sure to know that they were coming. Proceeding inside, they found nothing in the first two cells and then Dick's dead body in the third. He was face down lying in a crimson pool of his own blood, a weird looking chair standing ominously in the background.
Orwell checked his colleague for a pulse just to confirm the obvious and found none, so they quickly continued to search the basement for the perpetrator. Their flashlights fought against the ever present darkness but seemed to be losing the battle to the pitch black emptiness. Cell-after-cell they

found nothing until there was only one more to go of the thirteen down there.

Orwell couldn't stand the horrible stench which seemed to permeate the air everywhere like some vile animal farm full of dead carcasses and defecation. As he stepped inside the remaining cell, for some reason, a memory reformed in his mind of 1984, when he'd first joined the police academy. Huxley followed him through the door perceiving little as he did so due to the dim light afforded to them.

They both pointed their flashlights around the room and both ended up resting on a petite pretty blond girl who stood there naked before them carrying a shotgun. Unfortunately, it was currently pointed directly towards them. Pris fired the weapon and hit Orwell directly in the chest at close range and he died instantly before even making contact with the floor as he was thrown back by the blast.

Huxley bravely knew his world had come crashing down all around him and he was now alone; an island in a fast flowing stream of consciousness. Before he could turn properly to fire back at her, the girl fired again hitting him in the neck and face and he instantly felt nothing whatsoever besides a drifting movement upwards as he left his prone body behind him.

8.

It was late evening and Lauren was busy studying her findings and research. Unfortunately, she had been able to find out little about the *Order of Val Kyrie* except for the fact that they were most likely some weird devil-worshipping cult. Their emblem was three intertwining snakes set with emeralds. This was both on the dagger that she was currently studying a picture of and also supposedly on a ring belonging to the leader Andrew Murray.

Jess Anderson and Sarah Hurd of the Anderson case had both stated before their demise that they had witnessed this very ring and so too had Beth Maloney who had been released some days ago for psychiatric assessment and supervision due to a complete mental breakdown. Her symptoms were very similar in fact, to detective Lucas who had also been placed in the same facility.

As far as Lauren knew the dagger was still held in the evidence room at police headquarters and she pondered the possibility of removing it as well as paying a visit to Beth and Lucas to see if they could provide any extra valuable information. *What should I do?* After a few moments, her decision was made; she would get hold of the dagger and go and see both the still living witnesses. She checked her watch: two hours to go before she had to be at work for the night-shift.

Changing quickly into her police uniform she left her flat and headed out to see both Beth and Lucas figuring that she'd try and get hold of the dagger later, some time during her shift. She took with her the picture of it from the Anderson file just to confirm it was also, the one that Beth saw. Twenty minutes later, she reached the institution where

they were being held and after showing her credentials was led inside.
It turned out that Lucas was currently under heavy sedation as his mental condition seemed to be deteriorating day-by-day but Beth was luckily, still lucid enough for her to visit but only for a short while. A male orderly led Lauren towards her room and, after allowing her inside, restated the fact that she would only be allowed ten minutes with her. Beth was still under observation and clearly not very well suffering from both mental and physical exhaustion.
As he left, Lauren studied the young woman before her: she was curled up in a corner of the room squatting against the wall staring down at the floor. All the officer could see was that she had long dark hair tied back into a ponytail as she approached the whimpering female in front of her. Lauren knelt down beside her near to the wall so that hopefully they could converse in conversation.
"Hi Beth, my name's Lauren- I'm a police officer, do you remember me? I interviewed you for a short while at the station", she began.
The girl didn't reply but instead simply folded her arms more tightly around her legs to shield herself whilst still crying softly, disconsolately.
"Beth, I know it's hard for you as you've been through so much but I really need to talk to you about this dagger", she finished withdrawing the picture of it from her pocket and placing it under Beth's field of vision.
The girl whimpered once more but gradually as Lauren patiently waited, she began to open up. "That's the dagger I saw, the one the horrible man used to kill Megan and then he raped me!" she cried desperately.
"Listen Beth, I'm currently working on a case and it would really help me if you could..." Lauren began as the girl suddenly began to shriek violently and

uncontrollably in utter misery and despair. “I stuck it right in his chest for what he did to us!” she shouted. The male orderly quickly returned and asked Lauren to leave whilst he tried gently to console and calm his patient down.

Having no choice but to go, the officer headed out thinking, *well at least she confirmed it as the murder weapon.* She left the facility and headed for the station, as she knew that all staff were needed to work as much as they could manage due to the circumstances, and the horrific losses the whole department had suffered. Soon, she reached headquarters and headed inside, ducking around the police cordon and numerous members of the press who were still camped up outside.

Lauren wasted no time and headed for the evidence room. Reaching there, shortly afterwards, she chatted to the male officer on duty and pretended to be interested in him; flirting overtly in order to achieve her goal. After agreeing to a date with him, later on in the week, he let her have the dagger wrapped in its plastic evidence bag on condition that she bring it back the following day. He accentuated the fact that otherwise *his ass would be on the line.*

The demon controlling Pris headed back to cell three leaving the dead bodies of Orwell and Huxley where they were. Reaching there, he laughed as he discovered that officer Bukowski’s body too had returned and had fallen off the chair onto the floor in front of it. His whole body had been gored horrifically by some kind of animal with large teeth. The policeman’s blood added to the pool that was still around his partner.

Wasting no time, the demon pulled the chair away from the wall and placed it in the dead centre of the cell onto a demonic symbol he had quickly drawn on the floor. He then proceeded to fill the walls with numerous satanic signs as he followed the required rituals to hopefully enable some of his fellow demons to shortly pass through the portal that he had created. After performing several rites and incantations, he realised that it wasn't working; more blood sacrifice was required it seemed. *That shouldn't be a problem,* he thought knowingly as *their back-up should arrive any minute!*

Meanwhile, Lauren had hidden the plastic covered dagger in the bottom of her bag and left it by the corner of her desk. She then proceeded to help out as best she could to aid her colleagues in the aftermath of what had been a complete disaster. As soon as Kristen turned up, they'd head out for the streets and Willowbrook itself, as she had heard that there was yet another incident there, this very evening.

Two patrol cars screeched to a halt and turned their sirens off outside the main entrance to the old institution, parking alongside their colleagues vehicles that were clearly still inside, their blue lights still flashing. Wasting no time, the four officers headed inside the building, drawing their weapons and holding up their flashlights as they did so. Rapidly, they searched the ground floor but found nothing whatsoever and shortly afterwards, they all proceeded towards the stairwell.

Yet again, they decided to split up with a male officer and his female partner heading downstairs and the other two male officers going up to check the higher floors. Their flashlights darted around the stairwell as the proceeded in separate directions. All had to move cautiously, as it was really hard to see clearly in the insufficient light provided from their flashlights. The darkness seemed omniscient and powerful in the foreboding institution.

The two policemen reached the basement level and forced their way through the door, grimacing at the loud grating noise that it produced which invaded their space and echoed all around the dank, vile smelling confines of the pitch black darkness that threatened to engulf them. Cautiously, they proceeded inside with weapons drawn and flashlights desperately held up at shoulder level to illuminate their path.

They both gagged and grimaced at the smell as they carefully stepped down the corridor. The penetrating blackness all around them, served to conjure up all types of ghouls and ghostly images in their minds. Fighting their fear, they continued with adrenalin pounding through their respective bodies. They subsequently found the first two cells to be empty. Then, in the third, they discovered two fellow police officers were *down.*

The female partner immediately tried her radio but could get no signal. Her male colleague signalled for her to go back upstairs and reticently she left him alone down there. He heard her rushed footsteps echoing all around him as she left and then ascended the staircase. Standing still, he waited in cell three and looked around the room. A weird kind of chair had been placed in the centre on top of some kind of strange markings on the floor. Also, he could see the walls were covered with a multitude of symbols and drawings that he did not recognise.

In the background, somewhere nearby, he could hear a constant dripping noise that chilled him to the bone. His sixth sense told him to get out of there right now before it was too late, but he ignored it and continued to wait for his colleague to return, pondering the meaning of the symbolism before him. *I've never seen anything like it,* he thought, *what kind of weird shit it going on here?* His female colleague reached the ground floor and tried her radio again but just as she was about to speak she found herself gurgling and tasting her own blood in agonising pain. Then she noticed in the dim light, the end of a crimson blade protruding out of her chest. Soon afterwards, she felt nothing whatsoever except for a drifting motion whereby her spirit or essence appeared to be going somewhere else. Her last memory was unclear, but she thought she saw her own body fall to the floor and then lay motionless with a shadowy naked figure standing behind what used to be her.

Pris wasted no time and quickly withdrew the knife from the back of the dead officer. She turned the corpse onto its back and proceeded to cut into her chest vociferously with the blade until she had removed the officer's heart which was still beating weakly as she held it out in front of her. After a while, that stopped and she slunk back into the shadows still holding it.

Downstairs her male counterpart, officer Riggs was still staring around the room he was in, both flabbergasted and confused. *What the hell's going on here?* His thoughts were meandering all over the place and he felt weak and unsteady on his feet. The only available option to rest his weary body and soul was on the chair in front of him, so he walked over towards it and sat down.

The next thing he consciously recognised, after seemingly rushing through a swirling twisting vortex, was that he was in some kind of trench. Ahead of him were numerous soldiers lined up against the earthen wall. He looked down and could see that he too was dressed in a private soldier's uniform and in his hands he held an old fashioned one-shot rifle. Riggs had studied English history at high school and he immediately surmised that he was miraculously suddenly involved in a WWI campaign.

His memory was a bit vague but he instantly assumed that he was fighting on the side of the British as his fellow soldiers wore rounded helmets and not the weird pointed ones, he recalled of the Germans. In front of him, he watched as many of the lads pinned last letters and notes into the wall with their bayonets. Riggs suddenly realised frightfully that they were about to go *over the top*.

Nearby, he spotted what appeared to be a low ranking officer as he held a pistol as well as a whistle around his neck and he was currently barking orders out to everyone.

"Sir please, can I have a word?" Riggs asked his superior.

"Yes, what is it, private?" the man replied condescendingly in a posh accent.

Rigg's quickly thought over how he should address the officer in his mind and began with: "I think we're making a terrible mistake, sir. If we step out of this trench I know we'll all be killed- it'll be like mass suicide!"

"What do you mean you know?" asked the officer, confused.

"Sir, I mean the German's are bound to have our position covered by machine-guns. Also, why are we going over in broad daylight... at least we might have a chance at night!" Rigg's moaned.

"Orders are orders private... Fall in now unless you want to be shot as a deserter!" the officer stormed back at him.

"But sir, it'll be nothing more than a wasteful loss of life... If you send us over knowing we face certain death then, I'd say its more like a blood sacrifice for the devil-worshipping upper classes who most likely want to cull the population as well!" Rigg's cried back at him despairingly.

On hearing his words, the officer pulled out his pistol and aimed it directly at his face. "Fall in now or die as a deserter, you filthy coward!" he shouted.

Rigg's realised he could do no more and the game was clearly up. Strangely, he found that he was now going against his better nature and preparing for the assault. *Why wasn't he running away and getting the hell out of there?* He seemed no longer to be in control of his actions and could only watch as he joined his fellow soldiers against the wall.

Suddenly, the officer he had just spoken to blew his whistle and his comrades started to climb up the makeshift ladders, one after the other. Many were shot and fell backwards dead as soon as their heads protruded above the trench. His fellow soldiers continued going up the ladders anyway in numbers and finally a few seemed to make progress. Rigg's followed under the wistful gaze of his superior who was behind him and found himself in a conflagration of fire and explosions all around him.

Running towards the enemy trenches, he saw many of his comrades fall under the constant barrage of machine-gun fire but still they carried on. Rigg's managed to get half-way across no-man's-land when numerous bullets pierced his skull and he fell back dead into the mud. *Oddly, he had not even caught sight of an enemy soldier before he had been killed and his weapon had not been fired.*

Meanwhile, on the second floor of Willowbrook, the two other male officers, Gibson and White were checking around that particular level, searching room-by-room; the first floor had been empty, so they had continued upwards. After another fruitless search, they decided to join their colleagues in the basement. Heading back into the stairwell, they descended the stairs, moving slowly and carefully as visibility was limited under the dim glow of their flashlights.

As they reached the ground floor level, Gibson swore aloud, as his torch flickered briefly and then went out. He tried to shake it and reinsert the batteries using the glare from White's light as a guide but it still wouldn't work.

"Looks like the batteries have gone", he said aggrieved. "I've got some fresh ones in the car… you might as well head down to the others and I'll catch you up in a minute", he finished walking towards the exit. White nodded and continued his descent whilst Gibson went to fetch them.

Alone in the dark, White felt mildly nervous and afraid especially with only the dim glare of his flashlight to guide him. Still, holding his nerve, he continued down until he reached the basement door which yielded unwillingly with a horrible grating screeching noise. He paused for a second as the sound was so interminably loud that it reverberated around the basement corridor and cells for some time afterwards.

When silence resumed, White proceeded on and found that the first two cells were empty. Approaching the third one he called out, "Hey Riggs, Chaney where are you?" He waited but received no reply, grimacing as his voice echoed around the passageway. Entering the third cell, his heart nearly stopped as he was confronted by the horrific scene: two officers lay clearly dead on the floor in a pool of their own blood and Rigg's was sitting partially upright in the chair with two bullet-holes in his forehead.

His first instinct was to run and get the hell out of there but he quickly repelled this thought, chastising himself for his lack of courage and remained where he was. *After all, Gibson should be joining him any minute now*, he thought as though to convince himself and placate his emotions. He didn't recognise the dead officers on the floor and simply figured they must be on an alternate shift-pattern to him; consequently he hadn't seen them before. *Then again, they weren't easily identifiable, covered in all that blood,* he thought.

He walked over to one of the prone bodies nearest to him. Suddenly, he heard what sounded like a shotgun blast, coming from somewhere close behind him. Then he looked down to see his innards and intestines were hanging out of his gut before him as there was a gaping hole around his stomach area. Then White felt nothing as he fell to the floor, dead.

Kristen turned up at the department, ten minutes early as usual, for the nightshift and found Lauren at her desk. They exchanged greetings and immediately headed out towards their patrol car, as their sergeant had instructed them to go to Willowbrook to check on what was happening there. All he had said was that they had sent eight officers and no-one had yet bothered to call back in, except for the first call for back-up from the initial crews that had first arrived at the scene.

For some unknown reason, even to herself, Lauren took her bag with her and slung it behind her seat as something was telling her to take the dagger along, even though she was unsure of who or what. Kristen noticed her do so but didn't bother to say anything as their relationship was only just beginning to improve lately and she didn't want to *rock the boat.*

Lauren drove at a leisurely pace towards the old institution with a strange mixture of intuition and a sense of foreboding that she didn't bother to voice. She sensed unnervingly that something was wrong but then again, that old place had been playing on her mind since the first time she had been there. This feeling had only worsened with her research and now she found herself almost wishing she was somewhere else.

Gibson was just re-entering the stairwell when he heard the voluminous gunshot which reverberated and echoed off the walls all around him. *It sounded like some kind of shotgun but he couldn't be sure.* Wasting no time he rushed down the stairs and forced open the basement door, ignoring its loud groaning creak of protestation. Almost running now, he reached cell three and looked inside as the first two rooms he past, again were empty.

Shock and horror greeted him simultaneously in abundance. *Holy shit! Four officers down!* The floor of the cell was now a streaming vast pool of blood and Gibson had to step back to avoid treading in it. Shining the flashlight around the cell, he recognised his partner lying face down in the dark crimson pool of blood, ahead of him with a large wound in his back. *Fuck! I better call this in!* Reaching for his radio in the dim light he struggled to find the emergency push button as his hand was shaking so badly.

He forced himself to calm down, and was just about to press it, knowing it would immediately activate an emergency signal calling in all available units, he felt a tremendous force applied to the small of his back. Flying forwards into the air, he just happened to land directly on the chair in front of him which had been placed in the dead centre of the room. Time and space intermingled in a whirling vortex that he could not understand or comprehend as his being rushed towards the unknown.

Gibson regained consciousness to find that he was on a stage in front of a screaming and baying crowd, playing an electric guitar to a large an enthralled audience. He watched as his left hand moved rapidly over the six strings bending various notes with his fingers whilst his right was rhythmically sounding a beat. Soon, he found himself breaking into a solo after the lead singer had screamed his last vocal.

Now he was no longer just playing riffs, he appeared to be doing multiple trills, hammer-ons and pull-offs in a rapid but melodic harmony of intertwining notes and sound. The crowd were now becoming ecstatic and he found himself loving the experience; the adrenalin pumping through his veins in nervous excitement to create a mesmerising performance under the glare of the limelight.

Gibson quickly realised that he was not actually the one playing as he'd never picked up a guitar in his life and couldn't even play a note, let alone a chord. Even so, it was thrilling to be with this person, seemingly looking through his eyes and witnessing everything as he was, regardless of the fact that he was just a spectator. *What a thrill!* He thought thinking that he'd never experienced such a high in his life before.

Then the singer came back in and Gibson realised that the band he was in was some kind of hard rock with screaming groaning almost satanic sounding vocals and lyrics to match. The crowd too looked like a weird collection of vampires and freaks, all dressed in black, covered in tattoos, face paint or odd make-up. However, even though the overall sound was almost catatonic, they still seemed to love it. Luckily, though it turned out to be their final song as Gibson thought, it was really unpleasant to listen to.

The officer followed the band off stage to raucous cheers of appreciation from the baying crowd and they headed for the backstage dressing room. Here they proceeded to drink copious amounts of alcohol and take numerous drugs; especially cocaine and amphetamine based ones, such as speed, MDMA and the like. Gibson tried to abstain as much as he could but the other band members kept asking, *what the fuck's wrong with you tonight?* So he found himself forced to partake and shortly afterwards, he felt completely out of his mind.

What appeared to be their manager came in at one point and congratulated them all. Gibson found it hard to focus on his physical features because his vision was now so distorted and blurred but he could see the vague outline of a tall man. Strangely though, he seemed to be able to focus on small indistinct things that he probably wouldn't have noticed otherwise. Thus, the manager's ring that he was wearing on one hand came incredibly sharp into focus at one point even though the rest was a blur. It seemed to consist of three intertwining snakes that appeared to be set with emeralds and rubies for eyes.

It was just past 11.30pm and their manager told them to cool of the drugs for a while as they were all expected to be at tonight's ceremony and ritual at 2am the following morning. Everyone immediately agreed to do as he asked as he clearly had a presence and power over them, way beyond his job title. *What the hell are they on about?* Gibson pondered this as he sipped a beer. He also thought, *why on earth are we going to some kind of ritual at 2am? Something here was clearly not right; there seemed to be a strong satanic undertone to everything that they did* and he began to dread what he might have to witness later on.

9.

Lauren and Kristen pulled up outside Willowbrook's main entrance to find numerous squad cars parked out front. Quickly taking out their flashlights and drawing their guns they headed inside after Lauren had briefly delayed to get something form the back seat. Whilst Kristen had her back turned towards her, she had slipped the ornate dagger under her waist belt to hold it in place.
They immediately came across the corpse of a female officer who appeared to have her whole chest opened and her heart removed as there was clearly a bloody space where it should have been. Continuing onwards, they wasted no time checking any of the higher floors as the basement was definitely now going to be their first port of call. Reaching the stairwell, they descended into the omniscient dark with a sense of foreboding and adrenalin pulsing through their bodies. Immediately, they could sense something was up as eight of their colleagues had entered the building and yet they could hear no sound whatsoever, except for that constant dripping sound coming from somewhere out of view.
Lauren's spine tingled as they pulled back the heavy basement door which yet again, ground, grated and creak on both its hinges and the stone floor beneath. The hideous stench hit them fully as they entered the corridor, almost like a warning sign to keep out. The first two cells again were empty but the third, as always, proved to be where the nightmares lay. Shining their lights around the cell, they could see the corpses of four male officers. Most seemed to have died from what appeared to be shotgun or bullet wounds but one had died via lacerations to the throat.

Also, they noticed the chair had moved in position and was currently now resting in the dead centre of the cell. Underneath it was some strange symbolism and markings on the floor that they did not recognise or understand. Further, every wall had similar inscriptions and drawings that made no sense to either of them. However, they quickly conjectured that these were likely some form of *black magic.*

Leaving the cell, they checked the rest of those remaining down there and came across two further corpses; both male officers in cell thirteen. The two female partners felt utterly sickened and disgusted by what they saw; *none of their colleagues deserved to die like this.* They headed back to cell three and went inside to find the chair actually moving by itself backwards along the ground. It made a horrible grating charring sound against the stone floor as it did so which echoed and reverberated all around them. It finally stopped and rested still once more about two feet from the back wall.

"What the fuck?" exclaimed Kristen incomprehensibly, "That damn chair just moved by itself!"

"I know", whispered Lauren, "Let's get the hell out of here and call it in!"

"I'm right behind you partner- let's get going!" Kristen cried out anxiously as even for her this was one step too far.

Gibson found himself dressed in a dark robe, seated at one side of a wide rectangular chequered floor in what appeared to be a large cavernous space underground. He could see that there were possibly around fifty people seated around him and a similar number opposite. The two other smaller sides of the rectangle seemed to accommodate the higher ranking members of the order as they were sat on elevated chairs or thrones. He recalled through his blurred vision being led underground down a wide stone staircase but really not much else as the drugs he had taken previously had only just now began to wear off.

The officer felt a strange sense of foreboding and an unnerving feeling of disquiet as *clearly, something was going to take place here that was ultimately very wrong!* He considered his options but they seem strictly limited as *how could one individual battle against what appeared to be over a hundred? No, all he could do was play along and see what happened, otherwise he might find himself at the receiving end of some kind of punishment* as he sensed a dark satanic presence in their midst even though, he was not a spiritual man.

Lauren and Kristen headed from the cell and made their way down the pitch black corridor towards the exit with only the weak beams of their flashlights for guidance. Lauren was just passing the opening to cell two, with Kristen following closely behind her, when a naked girl stepped out of the shadows into the corridor from the cell ahead of them. She appeared to have blood stains covering various parts of her body and she was holding a shotgun that was pointed directly towards them.

Lauren instinctively dived out of the way into cell two just as Pris pulled the trigger. Kristen just managed to fire off a shot but unfortunately, the blast from the shotgun hit her squarely in the chest and she fell to the floor grimacing in agony. Her partner quickly aimed her gun around the doorway of cell two and saw that Kristen's aim had been accurate and the girl had been hit right between the eyes. Pris stood where she was in shock momentarily, before suddenly her now lifeless body slumped to the floor. A piercing inhuman shriek echoed down the corridor and rang out in the darkness, as the demon took flight from Pris' corpse.

Lauren rushed over to her partner but she had a large wound in her chest and was coughing up blood as she desperately tried to draw in breath. Kristen tried to say something to her but it just came out garbled and with blood gurgling in her mouth she collapsed and died whilst Lauren was desperately calling to her to hold on. She screamed aloud in despair as she lifted and cradled her dead partner in her arms.

Gibson watched as a man rose from a large throne, clearly their leader, and began to address the multitude. After greeting them all, he then began what appeared to be a satanic ritual performing various rites and incantations, as well as paying homage to what he referred to as their *Master*. Much of what he said, the officer failed to understand as most was in a language that resembled Latin but he couldn't be sure. This ceremony seemed to go on for hours. Then the dark congregation began to chant rhythmically in expectation of something to come, or so it seemed.

Suddenly, a girl screamed wretchedly as she was dragged by two guards carrying spears from the shadows and placed in front of their leader. She was slim and pretty with long blond hair and completely naked. The man must have been aroused by her as his robe instantly poked outwards around his groin area. He produced a dagger from a sheaf at his side which he held aloft to the increasing chanting of his followers which seemed to becoming more and more frenzied with each passing moment.

Gibson could barely bring himself to watch as the leader approached the naked girl who was now cowering before him. *Oh my God*, he thought, *what's he going to do?* Suddenly, the leader lowered the dagger to his side and called on a *brother* from the congregation to finish performing the ritual. He looked around amongst them and finally, having made his choice, he pointed directly towards Gibson, as all eyes turned upon him.

Having no choice but to get up, he stumbled down a few steps towards the leader in the now centre of the chequered floor. The man performed some kind of satanic prayer over him before quickly holding out the dagger towards him. Again, feeling somewhat spellbound, Gibson took hold of the dagger and regarded it. It seemed ornate and antique with a strange handle consisting off three intertwining snakes beset with emeralds. It shone malevolently in the glare given off by naked torches placed all around them.

The chanting of the congregation had begun once more and became more fervent as Gibson lifted the dagger up and stepped towards the naked girl in front of him. She screamed for mercy in a desperate plea that echoed and reverberated in the cavernous space. Almost bewitched Gibson held the blade to her throat as the followers all around became more frantic in both their swaying and chanting. The officer knew what they wished of him and to his utter dismay he felt compelled to do as they desired even though that was the last thing he wanted.

Desperately, Gibson tried to fight the urge to slit the girl's throat, clearly she was some kind of sacrifice, and the dagger began to shake slightly in his hand as he did so. He looked once more at the girl weeping on her knees below him and fought with all his might to stop himself doing what he felt compelled to do. The one thing that prevented him more than anything else, as he was not a religious man, was recalling his oath to *serve and protect* the public *not slaughter them*, in some *depraved*

sacrificial ritual. He finally had found the strength to do what he needed and as the satanic congregation watched he dropped the dagger on the floor in front of him where it clattered and reverberated until finally coming to a standstill.
The leader commanded him to do his duty and pick up the dagger but the officer would not and soon Gibson found himself stripped of his robe and held down in front of the leader by two guards who had appeared from the shadows. The chanting of the congregation again reached a crescendo as the man stepped forward towards them and quickly slit the girl's throat and then Gibson's in quick succession. The officer felt a momentary tremendous pain in his neck and then blissful nothingness as he seemingly floated upwards out into the ether.

Lauren finally placed Kristen's corpse gently on the floor with tears now streaming down her eyes as she did so. Her in-built sense of self-preservation was telling her to *get the hell out of there and as soon as possible!* Through her blurred vision she stumbled towards the basement door and had just about reached it, when it suddenly slammed shut in front of her. All around her a penetrating grating grinding sound echoed and reverberated off the walls which took a long while to dissipate in the dark dank confines of the cellblock.
She tried with all her might to open the door but it just wouldn't budge; it seemed welded shut at the hinges. Despairing now of her current plight, Lauren wandered what the hell to do; her mind a frantic mixture of fear and loathing. Just as she was trying to come up with an idea she heard a hideous grating noise coming from further down the corridor in front of her. She shone the flashlight in that direction but nothing materialised but the

sound still remained and it appeared to be getting, not only louder but coming closer towards her.
Petrified now, Lauren watched as the chair, moving of its own volition or so it seemed, emerged from cell three and turned to face her in the corridor. Warm pee trickled down her leg as it then proceeded to rise in midair in front of her and slowly but surely, fly towards her, suspended by nothing but thin air. *How could that be possible? This surely is just nothing but a bad dream? I need to wake up!* Such thoughts abounded around her brain as the chair approached.
Suddenly, the figure of a uniformed officer appeared on the chair in front of her. He looked at her with lifeless eyes and his head slightly resting to one side. Lauren could clearly see in the dim light given off by her flashlight, the large gash cut across his throat. The chair suddenly stopped, no more than five feet in front of her; the jerk causing the man's corpse to fall off it to the floor below. She was then overwhelmed by a dark satanic presence which made her hairs stand on end on the back of her neck.
This horrific evil spirit didn't reveal itself to her visibly but instead seemed to gather force as it swirled around her and suddenly she was lifted into the air and thrown onto the chair in front of her. Lauren couldn't believe what was happening, as her body was lifted from the ground by some unseen power and she flew for a few seconds through the air before colliding and landing on the chair. *This is just not possible and shouldn't be happening!* Before her conscious mind could assimilate and make sense of her thoughts and predicament, she felt herself rising up into a mystical swirling vortex that twisted turned and rushed her through it, into a blinding light in the distance.

Lauren awoke from what had appeared a mesmerising and incoherent dream in which her body or spirit had seemingly been flying through space and time itself, to find she was sat behind the wheel of a car in a vast car park. She could vaguely make out some buildings in the far distance and could clearly see a multitude of white lines that marked out hundreds and hundreds of parking spaces all around her. She got out and looked around and suddenly spotted a dark black sedan parked about fifty yards away from her.
As she looked at the vehicle in front of her, its driver's side door suddenly opened and a tall man in a dark black suit and tie got out and approached her in what appeared to be the hot midday sun which shimmered all around them. A few minutes later, he stood directly in front of her as she regarded him. He was handsome but gaunt with short cropped dark hair and immaculately dressed in a black suit, tie and matching leather shoes. Also, he wore a strange but remarkable ring on one finger consisting of three intertwining snakes beset with emeralds.
After a few moments he addressed her, "I believe you have something of mine?" he said nonchalantly. Lauren looked at him dumbfoundedly wandering what he meant. As she pondered his question, he seemed to reach forward and grab the dagger from her belt swiftly all in one movement. "This", he finished as he quickly swiped the dagger across her throat. She felt a tremendous pain flash through her mind but then nothing as she floated upwards; her last recollection was of the dark suited man and her body lying on the lot beside him.
The man slowly walked back to his car. Shortly afterwards he reached it and went to the back and opened the trunk. Inside it, he had a black briefcase which he carefully unlocked by first entering a combination and then a key. Once opened, it

revealed a shining highly polished ornate dagger with a handle comprising of three intertwining snakes beset with emeralds, nestled inside. Taking out a rag from the side of the trunk he wiped Lauren's blood off the blade of the dagger he was holding, before placing it inside the case.

The man looked down at the interior of the case and paused momentarily with satisfaction. Two identical daggers now sat side-by-side nestled within its plush interior. However, there appeared to be a third space which still remained empty; it looked as though it was awaiting a similar dagger to accommodate it. The man shut and locked the case and got in the car and drove off, leaving Lauren's corpse behind in the vacant lot.